CLAIBORNE COUNTY BREAKDOWN

Nine short stories inspired by old time folk songs

By Patrick Watts

I dedicate this book to my wife Judy S. Watts. She is a highly accomplished, published writer in her own right (pun intended). She helped me the most with this endeavor. That extended to technical support, inspiration and motivation. What a treasure.

TABLE OF CONTENTS

ACKNOWLEDGMENTS

Thank you, Jim Smoak, for two years of first rate banjo lessons. Those deepened my love for folk music considerably. They were the origins of the idea for this book.

Thank you, Dr. Marian with FirstEditing.com, for your editing work and for your kind comments of my book.

Thank you, Fiona Jayde for the cover. It very well compliments the words and tone inside.

Thank you, Judy, for all the technical advice, motivation and overall support. And thank you for loving me.

Here are nine short stories inspired by old time folk songs. My stories come most directly from the songs "Molly and Tenbrooks," "The Oxford Tragedy," "The Wexford Girl," "Molly Bawn," "Polly Vaughn," "The Johnson Boys," "Good Old Mountain Dew," "Dooley," "John Henry," "The Wreck on the C. & O.," "Silver Dagger," "Katy Dear," and "Cumberland Gap."

My stories include allusions to other songs as well, such as "Jimmie Brown the Newsboy" and "Groundhog." Names of most of the characters in my stories are names of characters from even more songs, such as Lucy Lee, Cindy, Katy Daly, Angeline Baker, Willie Moore, Jack Davy, and Rattler. Any fan of old time folk and bluegrass music will recognize many more songs and names.

Coal mining songs are innumerable. That industry has had a profound impact upon Appalachia. To reflect that, I used the industry as background for several stories. Additionally, my John Henry is a convict laborer in a mine rather than an employee of a railroad.

My stories are not straight restatements of the songs. I developed the situations and characters differently, as Calliope and Euterpe directed. The original songs about the horse race and the train wreck were based upon actual events. However, again, we had our own ideas about things.

One of those ideas was to have a core of characters that appear in all the stories to varying degrees. Some just lend a hand to help develop that particular story. Some have stories of their own that develop and resolve themselves across the entire collection. Although the stories are separate, they are interrelated by setting, characters and events.

At the end of this collection are the lyrics to several of the songs that inspired me. These are ones that relate directly to some of my stories and that are in the public domain. They are in turn based upon songs brought to Appalachia by immigrants from Great Britain. Artists performing traditional music will invariably alter wording or compose new verses as their own creativity dictates. Because of that I was unsure about the copyright status of the available versions of the other songs.

I composed all of the verses to the "Cumberland Gap" here.

God bless all folk musicians. God bless all musicians.

May 2014 P. Watts

A Horse Race

One of the many northern tributaries of the Powell River entered a valley, slowed down and meandered back and forth through the flat bottomland. Generations ago denizens of the area had built a road in the valley a ways from the water to avoid potential flooding and afford a straighter road. In one particular spot the road divided a big meadow about in half.

One bright and sunny afternoon in July 1889 a descendant of those road builders rode his mule along it in the meadow until he reached a herd of hobbled mules and horses to one side. He dismounted and added his own to the mix. Off the pommel of his saddle he lifted a corn meal sack containing something hard and cylindrical and flipped it over his shoulder. From there he merged into a group of three other men just beyond the animals. He greeted them all and from his sack half withdrew a shiny ceramic demijohn.

All his new friends smiled and nodded. Two flipped the demijohn onto their shoulders and connected its mouth to theirs.

Nearby an old man holding a baby boy in one arm and a basket loaded with carrots and rhubarb with the other, greeted another old man holding a lumpy burlap sack.

The man with the sack pulled from it a big turnip by its bushy green top to show off.

The men exchanged carrots and rhubarb for turnips. Then they tried their best to engage the infant in conversation, shaking its hands, chucking its chin and cooing.

Further on two thirtyish women greeted each other with hugs. They disengaged and admired each other's cotton print dresses and complimentary shawls and bonnets.

One introduced the other to a young girl by her side, who maintained a tight grip on the adult's dress with one hand and maintained a tight grip on the thumb of her other hand with her mouth.

The adults looked around them and decided the spot where they stood would suffice. They spread a quilt on the ground, set down their slat-sided baskets and set up to enjoy a picnic.

Two boys galloped by pretending to ride horses. They weaved around an assortment of picnickers, handcarts loaded with produce, canvas shelters protecting handmade clothes, household accessories and toys, and larger tents sheltering families. They reached a long table made with boards on saw horses loaded with fried chicken, smoked ham, roast venison, pots of beans, corn and greens, bowls of apples and pears and plates of cookies, pies and cakes. Here they stopped to feed.

After loading their plates they sat on a bale of hay next to a skinny boy aged about twelve wearing thin ragged clothes working his way through a pile of chicken wings. They all ate to a reel played by a woman with a concertina and an ancient man with a fiddle.

In front of them all, four young couples twirled through a set dance barefooted in the grass.

Two fiftyish men who had been strolling through the whole conclave stopped briefly to enjoy the music. One of the men wore a well-worn brown striped three-piece business suit and bowler. The other wore equally worn brown jean clothes, a flat-crowned slouch hat and a holstered Colt Navy .36.

The farmer type replied to a query by the businessman. "Truth be told, Squire, I aint axin ter be re-appointed. John air a-comin home in bout a month or so from werkin them thar boats on the Cummerlin River. He an Lucie Lee plan ter marry soon after that. All I wanter do is werk that thar farm wit em.'"

"A month. Well, Luvin, ye bin a tolerble good gov-mint sarvint. This here corner o Clay-burn County will be a-missin yer."

His name was spelled <u>Louvin</u>, but everyone he knew always called him <u>Luvin</u>. "This here corner o Clay-burn County will be gittin long fine thout me. I dun wore out a hunnert hoss shoes an nothin e'er happint roun here." He cupped his revolver's grip with his right hand. "Why, I ne'er e'en had call ter draw this here weepon on anyone."

"That thar Ainglish feller outer Middlesboro bin ter see yer?"

"Shore has. He 'lowed as our lan' aint got the right kinder rock er some sech. Ennyways, I aint minded ter sell. Borned and raised thar. Lucie Lee too. Naw, we'll stay put."

"That thar air a comfort. Things air a-changin roun here too fas fer my likin." The Squire nodded toward the distance. "Yer nephews thar, decide what theys a-gonter do bout Mr. Davy's offer?"

"Not as I knows on."

Both turned their attention to two handsome young men in their mid-twenties near the far edge of the crowd. They wore frayed brown jean overalls and scuffed brogans. They worked to implant a split cedar fence post next to the road.

Matthew Johnson, the one with the medium complexion and medium brown hair, held the post straight up.

His younger brother Mark, the one with a constellation of freckles over his face and hair on the red side of auburn, stamped the ground around the base of the post. After that he pulled a wad of sisal bailing twine out of a pocket, found an end, and gave that to Matthew. He unraveled the wad even more and walked across the road with it to another fence post already set directly opposite the other.

Both boys carefully laid the twine over the tops of both posts across the road.

Throughout this process, as the boys turned this way and that, two girls looking a few years younger stood close by and sidestepped back and forth to stay within direct line of sight of the boys. Both held mugs and every once in a while, when it appeared they'd caught the eye of one of the boys, they'd proffer one.

The boys paid them no mind whatsoever until their task was complete.

At that point the girls got real close and stuck the mugs nearly under the boys' chins.

They accepted, nodded a perfunctory thank you, chugged the contents, returned the mugs and then picked up their shovels, turned and walked away.

The girls did not follow. They just looked at each other then headed toward the long table of food.

It appeared to Louvin the girls were stomping a little as they walked. He shook his head.

The Squire pointed in another direction. "Yander comes a feller that Lucy Lee'll be wantin ter meet."

Louvin immediately picked him out in the crowd even though he was about a head shorter than him. He was in his early twenties. He had a fresh, close haircut and was dressed in new Methodist Episcopal clergy garb that was a size too large for him. He gripped a big shiny new Bible tightly to his chest with his left hand. As he promenaded through the crowd, he greeted some of the people with what appeared to be admonitions. He continued straight on to Louvin and Squire Bateman.

Squire Bateman spoke. "How air ye a-likin our little mountain randy-voo, Parson?"

The Parson replied in a New England accent. "Quite lovely. Lovely indeed."

"Luvin, this here is our new circuit rider fer these here parts, Jeremy Brown. Parson, this here is Constable Luvin Reilly."

Louvin extended his right hand and Parson Brown enveloped it with virtually no force at all and held it motionless. "Constable, I see men here with money in their hands. I suspect gambling. I am sure you would want to know about that."

Louvin slid his hand out of Brown's and looked at Bateman.

Brown likewise looked at Bateman. "And I expect the Justice of the Peace to prosecute to the fullest extent of the law."

This exhortation had no effect on Bateman's sunny disposition. "Jes folkses as air minded ter notch up the hoss race sum, Parson."

4

"A nefarious pastime that brings out the worst in people."

Louvin wanted to change the subject. "Er, Parson, ye air a-settin up in the chapel yander in the dale?"

"That is correct. Worship services on Sunday and, while I am traveling, school on weekdays."

"School, too?"

"That's right, Constable. My wife is your new teacher. You see, this whole region is going to experience a renaissance. Many very bright and charitable people are interested in improving the lives of its inhabitants. Industry is moving in to improve their material well-being. Churches and schools are coming in to improve their minds and souls. It will be a splendid demonstration of how government, business and the church can work together to uplift an entire culture."

"Gov-mint an bizness a-werkin tergether?"

"And the church. We all have our work cut out for us. But the end result will be a marvelous enrichment of Appalachia. Similar endeavors have been highly successful throughout the world. Of course, the local courts and constabulary have an important role, too, maintaining a safe environment for people to enjoy the substantive and spiritual wealth we will bring."

"Well, now. Shore preciate everone wantin ter hep us out sa much. Never knowed we was a-needin such."

"Naturally, there is resistance. It is a vast change from what you are used to. It is hard for you to conceive of the improvements. But, once you experience the benefits, you will surely embrace them."

The Squire pulled out his pocket watch from his vest and looked at it. "Oh, s'bout time." He looked up and off. "Matt! Mark! S'time! Git everone offen that thar road!"

Parson Brown looked up and off in the opposite direction. "I see a group of men over there who appear to be imbibing something out of a sack. Constable, you would not mind if I speak to them?"

Louvin looked back behind him then back at Brown. "Er. No, Parson. I reckon not. If ye air a-minded ter."

Parson Brown strode off toward the group draining the corn meal sack.

In the distance a gunshot popped.

Everyone except Brown looked in that direction. Then everyone except Brown and the three very restless men he was preaching to migrated into two groups, one behind each fence post.

Well up the road out of sight of the crowd two horses raced nose to nose. One was a palomino; the other was a dark bay. Their heads bobbed; their eyes bugged.

The palomino pulled ahead.

All the people looked up the empty road, shielding their eyes and craning their necks. Absolutely everyone shifted from one foot to the other.

Horse mouths slung slobber; horse necks gushed lather.

The palomino extended her lead by half a length.

In the middle of one group of people three men huddled together. The short one scribbled numbers onto a scrap of paper with a stubby lead pencil. The other two tapped the short one's chest with fists of money as they watched the road.

Someone shouted, "Here they come!" and everyone leaned toward the voice. Those in the back of the crowd hopped for a better view.

The three men Parson Brown was preaching to just left him in mid-sentence and ran to the nearest group by the road.

Brown followed them, still talking.

The horses came into sight of the spectators and mayhem ensued. "Aaah!" "Yeees!" Nooo!"

The tip of the palomino mare's tail flicked the bay stallion's nose.

Her rider, middle-aged, dressed in brown jeans, and straddling an old western saddle, flailed her backside with a hickory switch.

The rider of the bay, a younger, clean-shaven fellow with thick black hair, attired in a tailored European riding habit, hovered over a polished English saddle and tortured his steed with a braided leather riding crop. The worried look on his face was obvious even to the folks in the back of the crowd.

Twenty feet away from the finish line the palomino shrieked a heartrending neigh and collapsed head first into the road.

Her rider cartwheeled into the cedar post in front of them.

The spectators shouted their dismay. "Oooh!"

The bay ripped through the bailing twine and finally stopped near the herd of his lesser bred kindred farther down the road.

The people slapped backs, punched arms, hugged, cheered or cried as the fate of their favorite dictated. They re-divided. Some circled the downed palomino and some chased after the dark bay. Some crowded the short man with the scrap of paper and stubby pencil.

Louvin rushed to the palomino's rider who was gingerly rolling over to sit up. "Earl! Air ye hart!?"

Earl's hair, face and clothes were loaded with dirt. He sat there assessing damage. "Uh. Nuthin broke, I reckon. Hep me over ter Molly."

Louvin lent a hand.

Earl gasped and grunted as he rose to a slightly stooped stance. He limped over to his horse.

She lay on her side wheezing.

Just a few onlookers remained.

Earl carefully sat down, scooted his lap under his horse's head and stroked her ear. "Ye fer sartain luv ter run, gal. Run like hell broke loose this here time. Dun ye'sef in. I luv ye fer tryin, though." He looked up. "Will ye take keer o 'er, Luvin? I gots ter settle 'counts wit Mr. Davy."

"Awright. ... Oh. ... Uh, ye shore?"

"Lookit er, Luvin. She air nigh onter pegged out awready."

Louvin reset his hat and rubbed the back of his neck. "Ah. Reckon yer right. Okay." He shook his head. "Law, what a clammity, Earl. What air ye gonter do?"

"Don' rightly know. Aint figgered that part out yit. Gots no money. No hoss. Now, no lan'. Mos' probly have ter move up yander ter Pike County wit Betsy's kin. Law, I shore hate that idee. Hardest part'll be splainin ter Betsy what I dun. This'll try her sum-thin fierce."

As he talked Earl slowly stood, gasping between sentences. He left Louvin and limped toward the crowd surrounding the big bay horse and its rider.

Jack Davy had led his horse into the shade of a tree. He stood on the ground, facing the animal, holding its reins and raking his fingers through its tangled mane. He spoke to no one in particular in an English accent. "Magnificent thoroughbred. Impeccable lineage. Beat a train in Memphis last month."

Awestruck onlookers behind him nodded.

Pastor Brown walked up beside Davy. He now had his Bible tucked high up under his left arm. He stroked the horse's rump. "Father has thoroughbreds. Never seen one like this before. He's got the nerve and the blood."

They heard one of the onlookers say, "Sorry bout Molly, Earl," and both turned.

Davy took Earl's right hand in both of his and pumped it a couple of times. "Damn fine race! You had me! What happened?"

Earl winced from the handshake. "Muster knowd what was at stake. Aint ne'er seen her run like that afor. Had a stroke."

"Ahh. Bloody tough luck, that. Er. Shall we, ah, settle up? Your J.P. has the deed."

Earl nodded.

Both left Pastor Brown to worship Davy's horse and walked over to a knot of people with Bateman and the short man with the paper and stubby pencil holding forth in the middle. They were all at the end of the long table. The chicken, ham and venison had been pushed aside to clear a spot.

When he noticed them approaching Bateman pulled out two envelopes from inside his jacket. He handed the much thicker one to Davy and pulled a folded paper out of the other. He carefully unfolded that, perused it a moment then flattened it out on the table. He pulled a fountain pen from inside his jacket and uncapped it. He pointed to a line on the paper with his pen and looked at Earl.

Earl took pen in hand and signed his name.

A gunshot nearby caused him to jerk the last letter.

Not long after that Louvin, Earl, Matthew and Mark started digging a large hole next to the dead horse and everyone else returned to eating, drinking, dancing and catching up with neighbors and kinfolk.

2

The Oxford Tragedy

The black water of the millpond precisely reflected the clear blue sky and surrounding trees. The flora remained wet and shiny from the rain last night. A few trees suggested the coming of fall.

A snow-white down feather sat high and dry on the water's surface. Its fingers reached up to collect the warm sun. A puff of air pushed it into a slow drift toward the dam. It picked up speed. It entered a wooden trough built into the dam. It sped atop swift water along the entire length of the race and disappeared as the water poured over and drove the big water wheel. It reappeared in the pool below the wheel, soaked and broken.

Inside the mill a young man with black hair, black eyes and black disposition watched whole corn slide from a hopper, through a chute, into the center of grindstones and emerge from their sides as meal. Even though a pretty girl with blonde hair and dark brown eyes stood beside him, he never took his eyes off the machinery.

The turning stones, cogs and shafts sounded like a constant roll of thunder all around them.

She smiled and spoke to him over the loud rumble. "Law, Johnny, ye gots ter quit yore jealous ways. I luv ye. I aint took up with any uther."

"That true?"

"Gospel true!"

"What about that thar Ainglish feller? I seen ye wit im at Eli's las week. Ye was actin parful frienly."

"He was jes bein perlite. I was obleeged ter be th' same. He wants ter buy Paw's lan'. He bin a-sweet talkin me an Maw." She cut eyes away. "Nuthin ter talk bout."

Johnny looked into the hopper and rapped it hard on the side with a hand. "That thar air the last o yore Paw's corn. I'll bag it up an be out directly."

The girl sighed, but wrapped both her arms around Johnny's arm nearer to her. "See yer Sunday?"

"I reckon."

"We gonter talk bout the weddin?"

"Shore."

She smiled, gave him a peck on the cheek and departed.

Soon after, Johnny exited the mill carrying a full burlap bag over his shoulder. Just outside the door he saw something ahead of him and stopped dead still.

He saw an older man sitting in the seat of a buckboard wagon. That man was watching his girl standing beside the wagon cradling a huge bouquet of wild flowers in one arm and extending her free hand out to the Englishman Jack Davy. Davy was bending way down from the saddle of his thoroughbred, holding her hand in his and kissing it.

The girl noticed Johnny, jerked her hand back and quickly climbed into the wagon beside the man.

Davy glanced at Johnny but otherwise ignored him and spoke to the man sitting in the wagon. "That is the best I can offer, Mr. Dean. May I expect an answer soon?"

Johnny reached the rear of the buckboard, dumped the bag into the back next to four others and glowered at his girl.

She kept her eyes on the bouquet, nervously picking off dead leaves.

Mr. Dean said, "Me an the mizzuz hez gots ter think on this a might more. Give us a few days. Ye ready, Flora?"

"Yes, Paw."

Mr. Dean turned to face the rear of his buckboard. "Thank ee, Johnny. See yer Sunday?"

"Shore!"

Mr. Dean flicked the reins attached to the horse collared to his wagon. "Git up!" They all drove away and up a slope.

Jack Davy still ignored Johnny and cantered off in the same direction but kept some distance from the Deans.

Johnny kicked a puddle of water in the road and stomped back into the mill.

Mr. Dean drove his buckboard from the crest of the slope towards a crossroads a short distance away. At the intersection to their left was a wood frame building with a covered porch. A sign on the front wall above the porch roof floridly pronounced, "Eli Parch Mercantile." To their right was a single pen log cabin with a double door. Through that they could see and hear a large fire, puffing bellows and ringing steel. The fire silhouetted the blacksmith Charlie Waggoner banging a hammer onto a horseshoe over an anvil.

Outside a skinny boy about aged twelve sat on a barrel closest to the door. He was dressed in thin ragged clothes. His feet were bare. Beside him an ancient mule dozed against the wall. The boy waved at Mr. Dean and Flora. As they passed they returned the courtesy.

. . .

The shadows beside Charlie's and Eli's buildings were long.

Eli stepped out onto the front porch of his store and began tidying up for the new day. He waved at Mr. Dean and a woman of similar age across the street, who sat in Dean's buckboard parked in front of Charlie's.

They were dressed in their Sunday best, which was not that good, comparatively.

On his horse Constable Louvin Reilly approached Mr. Dean and the woman from in front of them. About two lengths away he waved at Eli, who waved back, and greeted the people in the wagon. "Jeb, Liza, what brings yer here ter the settlemint sa arly?"

Liza wiped her nose with a lace hanky, sighed and looked away.

Jeb wrapped an arm around her shoulders. "Flora air missin, Luvin. She'n Johnny set out a-walkin las evenin after supper an they dint come back. We went on ter bed whilst they were out an dint know she wasn't back til this mornin. Her bed aint bin slept in."

"Dint see Johnny, neither?"

"Nawsir."

"Look roun yore place?"

"Yep. Nigh onter half mile roun."

"Mebbe she went wit Johnny ter his place. Bin thar, yit?"

Jeb and Liza stiffened a little at this suggestion. "Nawsir."

"Reckon they 'loped? Johnny's bin a-courtin Flora fer quite a spell now."

Liza sobbed into Jeb's coat at this suggestion.

Jeb said, "I air a-thinkin no, Luvin. Flora was mighty keen on a charch weddin."

Louvin reset his hat and rubbed the back of his neck. "Uhm, sorry, Jeb, Liza. Les haid fer yore place rat now an look roun sum more." He maneuvered his horse to beside Jeb and headed in the same direction. They all rode away.

Eli continued to sweep his porch, all the time watching the trio depart.

Jeb, Liza and Louvin rode up and stopped in front of a neatly kept single pen log cabin. Farm implements rested in a row along the front wall. Two beehives hummed at a corner. They all debarked.

Jeb said, "Liza, I air a-thinkin Luvin would like a mug o fraish hot tea."

Liza nodded and entered her home.

Louvin said, "Thank ee, Liza." Then to Jeb, "Whar all'd yer go this mornin?"

"Actially don' recall. Jes walked roun an roun. Not really thankin."

Louvin surveyed the surroundings and pointed. "Well, les go down that thar road long o yore cornfiel'."

Both walked off together down two parallel strips of bare earth separated by a strip of grass. It ran along a small field recently harvested of corn. As they did, both looked up, down and side-to-side.

The wagon road ended at the other end of the cornfield and by the bank of a little river. Both men arrived there still looking around.

Suddenly Louvin grabbed Jeb's arm and stopped. He pointed to the ground. "Lookit how that thar grass air mash-ed down roun thar. An how that thar dirt air all de-sturbed." He looked around some more. "Stay thar, Jeb. Lemme look long here a minit."

Jeb obliged.

Louvin followed a trail of disrupted grass and dirt to the riverbank. He studied the ground there. "Fraish boot prints in the mud long the water here." He eased down the bank to water's edge and continued to examine the bank until he spied something there. He picked up a stout piece of hickory deadfall and examined it. "Looks like blood on this here stick!" Louvin looked back up at Jeb.

Liza was there, too. She shrieked, dropped the basket with the jug of tea and mugs and ran back up the trail toward her cabin.

The men just stood and watched her.

The shadows around the buildings of the settlement were gone.

A few people and animals loitered about Eli's and Charlie's.

A mule trotted up the road that intersected the main road and ran alongside Eli's store. A few feet of frayed rope dangled from its bridle. It passed in front of Louvin as he reached the intersection on his horse.

As he passed the intersection a man carrying a coil of rope with a frayed end passed behind him running after the loose mule.

As Louvin approached the blacksmith's his nephews Matthew and Mark Johnson and their dog Rattler ran up from the big shade tree beside it. Both boys were flushed and sweaty.

Matthew said, "Uncle Luvin, Uncle Luvin, we found us a daid gal!"

"Yeah, in the river nigh whar we laid sum traps." Mark pointed off into the distance.

"Ye reco'nize er?"

Matt said, "Naw. She was on t'other side. Face in the water."

"I gots ter fotch er out. I'll be a-needin yore hep."

Mark pleaded, "Naw, please, Uncle Luvin. Don' make me do that. I aint a-wantin ter touch no daid gal!"

Matt concurred, "Me neither! Don' make us do that."

Louvin sighed. "Can yer leastways show me whar she is?"

"I'll take yer thar, but I aint a-touchin er."

"Awright, awright, awright."

While they were talking Louvin reached the hitching rail in front of the blacksmith's. He dismounted and dropped the reins over the rail.

The hickory stick he took from the riverbank stuck out of his saddle bag. He retrieved that and started toward the door of the blacksmith's. "I gots ter set this here stick inside, an git sum rope. An git a wagon." He pointed to the big tree beside the shop. "You-uns jes set thar in the shade an rest easy till I git back." He entered the shop and the other three went over and plopped down, backs against the tree trunk.

At the bank of the river Mathew, Mark, Rattler and Louvin stood looking for several minutes across at the dead girl tangled up in a fallen tree.

Louvin held a large coil of rope and a pair of brown jean trousers. He wore no weapon. "Current air right swift here. We kin loop this rope roun that thar tree." He pointed upstream. "I'll loop this roun my ches an wade a-crosst whilst you-uns take holt a t'other end an pay it out as I go. If I slip, haul me back in."

They all moved upstream to the tree. Louvin looped the rope around the tree once and tied a bowline in the end. He slipped that over his head and under both arms.

As Louvin pulled some boot laces out of his pocket and tied the top of the spare trousers closed, Mark said, "If we gots ter haul ye back in this current, ye'll shorely go under."

As Louvin tied off the hems of both legs, he said, "I hope this'll pre-vent that." Before cinching the second leg up tight, he blew into it for a while, filling the pants full of air. Then he closed that leg tight. He wrapped the legs around his torso, tied them together with loose ends of the boot laces and brought the waist around to his chest with the legs under his arms. He then proceeded into the water.

The boys looked at each other and grinned, then took the rope, easing it out as Louvin moved into the water, heading farther upstream against the current.

In waist-high water Louvin stumbled and fell forward but the denim life vest supported him.

The current moved him downstream.

The boys hauled in some rope.

Louvin thrashed around a bit until he regained his feet and balance. "I air awright. Keep a-goin." He continued on into chest-deep water. Here, he had trouble keeping his feet on the bottom of the stream; his personal flotation device worked so well. He flailed his arms to keep his balance and move forward.

The current pushed him farther downstream.

He reached shallower water on the other side, close to the tree and girl. He waded over and turned her bruised face up out of the water. To the boys he called, "It air Flora Dean!" To himself he said, *Laws a mercy. What a turrble thang this be.*

He disentangled Flora from the branches of the tree, gently eased her over his shoulder and started upstream along the bank on her side, one arm over her and the hand of his other arm holding onto the rope. He entered the water well upstream of the tree.

As he retreated, the boys hauled in the slack.

In the chest-deep water Flora's weight kept Louvin from floating. However, the extra drag nearly toppled him over. He had to face the current and rely on the rope to keep him upright.

All the extra pressure required Matt and Mark to dig in as well.

Louvin shifted Flora around to keep her head and shoulders out of the water as high as possible. He cocked his head back to keep his nose as high as possible. Then he crab-walked to the bank. He staggered up and out and carried Flora over to a buckboard wagon. He laid Flora in the back.

Matt and Mark dropped the rope and followed a respectable distance behind.

Louvin looked over Flora's cut and bruised face and head. He looked closely at one gash in the side of her head and picked out a piece of tree bark. He walked over to the seat of the wagon, withdrew a saddlebag from underneath it, withdrew from that an envelope and dropped the piece of bark into the envelope. He returned it to the bag and the bag to the floorboard of the wagon.

"What happint to er, Uncle Luvin?" Mark asked.

"Beat an drownded."

"What sort o cussed varmint would do sech a thang? *Could* do sech a thang?" Matt added.

"I gots a idee . . . . Well, les put out fer the settlemint." Louvin spread a canvas tarpaulin over Flora and mounted the wagon and sat in the driver's side.

Matt walked over to a saddled mule.

Mark retrieved and coiled the rope and joined Matt.

Louvin looked back at them. "Who air ridin wit me?"

Both boys looked at Louvin then at the back of the wagon, then at each other. They remained in place.

"I declar!"

"We kin ride tergether on this here mule." Mark said.

"Suit yersef!" Louvin turned around to face forward and took up the reins.

Matt took a deep breath. "Mark, ye ride Grant; I'll ride wit Uncle Luvin."

"Okay."

Matt climbed into the front of the wagon and sat next to Louvin.

Mark looped the coiled rope over a shoulder and mounted the mule.

They all started off.

Rattler zigzagged nose down just ahead of them all.

Louvin rode up on his horse to a single pen log cabin, this one accessorized outside similarly to Jeb and Liza's. It was nowhere near as tidy as theirs, though. He stopped near the front door. "Johnny Oxford! … Johnny, it air Luvin Reilly. I come ter ax ye sumthin."

A middle aged woman opened the cabin's door and stepped out. She was dressed for working in the field. She looked as though she had worked in the field for sixty straight years.

"Hello, Mizz Oxford. Johnny here? I gots ter have a word."

"Afternoon, Con-stable. He air patchin the roof on the barn a-hint here. Ye kin go roun thar." She indicated one side of her cabin.

"He bin here all day?"

"Yessir. He come home real late las night mighty de-sturbed. Had blood on 'is shirt. 'Lowed as is nose'd bin a-bleedin. I said it 'peared ter be too much blood fer that, but he jes grabbed is haid an wailed. I warshed is face an wropped is haid. He waked me up more'n oncet a-hollerin out in is sleep. Bin porely all this day. I bin frettin over im considerable."

"Thank ee, Mizz Oxford."

Louvin rode around the way Johnny's mom had pointed. He found Johnny atop the roof of the barn. "Greetins, Johnny."

Johnny looked up from his shingles. He had dark circles under his bloodshot eyes. He resumed tacking a shingle in place. "Lo, Mr. Reilly."

"Johnny, I want yer ter come back ter the settlemint wit me."

"Gots ter patch this here roof!"

"Right now, Johnny. Yer mam said yer could go."

After a long pause, "Awright! Awright!" He gathered up hammer, nails and cedar shingles and plopped them all into a wooden box. He climbed down a ladder from the roof.

"Thank ee, Johnny. I'll wait here whilst ye saddle up yore hoss."

"She's in the pasture back here." Johnny disappeared around a corner of the barn. Less than a minute later he charged from behind the barn on his horse and galloped onto the trail leading away from his mamma's cabin.

"Dangit, Johnny! Stop!" Louvin heeled his horse and started after him. "Stop, I tell ye."

Johnny disappeared down the hill.

Louvin followed but never saw Johnny again. He came to a fork in the trail. One way led back toward the settlement. The other led to higher ground up the mountainside. "He shore aint gonter go ter the settlement." Louvin headed for the higher ground. After two hours he gave up and went back to Johnny's cabin. Maybe Nellie Oxford would know where her son might run to.

He got back to the settlement still wondering where to find Johnny. As far as Nellie knew Johnny never went anywhere except the mill, home and Flora's.

The skinny boy was sitting on his barrel outside the blacksmith's with his mule. Charlie was out there too. Both watched Louvin approach. Once Louvin was close enough, Charlie hollered, "Thar be a parful disturbament yander ter the mill!"

"What?"

"That durn fool Johnny Oxford's got that thar Ainglish feller in thar."

"What!?"

"Come a-tearin inter here on is hoss. Reined in sa hard he bout broke the critter's neck. Jumped off an lan-ned a solid kick ter Mr. Davy' hoss yander in front er Eli's. Run inter Eli's an come out directly wit Mr. Davy by his coat collar, jes a-squirmin an a-squeelin. Whupped im up side the haid a coupler times alls the while a-draggin im down ter the mill."

"He have a weapon?"

"Dint see one. Dan'l Miler run up from the mill a-cussin an a-sayin Johnny dun run im out wit a grain shovel."

"Whar air Dan'l now?"

The owner of the mill came out of Charlie's lightly rubbing a red goose egg on his forehead and carrying one of Charlie's hammers. "I air gonter show that boy how ter buss a haid!"

"Ye aint gonter do no sech thang!"

Eli and a customer trotted from across the road. "Louvin, that thar Johnny Oxford went plum crazy in my store! Chased that Mr. Davy roun in thar till he cotched im by is coat tail an punched im in the back. Then drug im out a-kickin an a-hollerin. Both strode my merchandise all o'er the place in the process!"

"Reckon I better go on down thar. Jimmie go an tell Mizz Oxford ter come down hyar."

The skinny boy smiled and mounted his mule from the barrel. "Yessir." He flapped the reins to urge his animal to wake up and flapped them again to urge the animal to move.

"Jimmie, take my hoss." Louvin dismounted and walked his horse next to Jimmie.

Jimmie stood up on the back of his mule and stepped onto the horse. He sat, took the reins from Louvin and sped up the road.

"Awright, everbody, jes stay put." Louvin made for the mill.

Everyone followed him.

Everybody stopped at the edge of the stream where two others stood.

One greeted Louvin. "Con-stable, I gots two sacks o meal in thar!"

The other said, "Mine air in thar, too!"

To these two Louvin said, "Jes git easy, whilst I try an talk ter Johnny." To the mill he called, "Johnny!? Johnny Oxford!"

The door at the second story opened and crashed against the side of the building. Johnny stood there with Jack Davy. Jack wore a rope knotted around his neck. Johnny gripped it at the knot.

Jack spoke first. "Constable, shoot this lunatic!"

Johnny jerked the rope to discourage Jack from talking. He said, "I air gonter hang im outer this here door!"

Everyone down on the ground sucked in a short breath.

Louvin called out. "Johnny, yer awready in a heap o truble! No call ter comply-cate yore life enny more!"

"Shore caint add ter what air a-comin ter me!"

Eli asked, "What air he jowin bout?"

"Kilt Miss Flora."

Everyone took in another short breath.

Louvin kept watching Johnny. "Johnny, ye might jes spen time in jail fer Flora. Ye'll hang fer Mr. Davy."

Davy squirmed and Johnny jerked the rope again. "My life aint worth a-savin! Bin a heap o truble fer everone ever since I was bornded!"

Miler spoke. "That thars fer sartain. Beat his pap half ter death. Come hyar fum Hancock ter git away fum his pap's famly."

"Johnny, thars always hope! Sumtimes it takes a while fer a feller ter fine hissef."

"I air dun wit that. I air tarred."

"Ye gots ter hurt Mr. Davy fer that?"

"He dun took fum me th'onliest thang I ever keered fer. Th'onliest one what was a-heppin me 'fine mesef' as ye say."

"I air a-thinkin ye air wrong bout that, Johnny. Everbody roun hyar knows Flora luved yer. She warnt took up with Mr. Davy."

Davy concurred. "To think I would bother with the likes of her is preposterous. Poor, uneducated. There is no one and no thing around here I find attractive, eckkk!"

Johnny cinched up the rope around Davy's neck.

The one with the two sacks of meal yelled, "Carnsarned varmint!"

Dan'l Miler threw Charlie's hammer. He threw hard and high but it still fell short, hitting the side of the mill about ten feet below Johnny and Davy. The boom echoed around the mill and dam and stirred everyone up even more.

Johnny threw the loose end of the rope over the beam sticking out of the wall above the door, caught it as it swung back and hauled in the slack.

Davy writhed and thrashed and slapped at Johnny to absolutely no avail. Johnny was much stronger than him. The rope was tight around his neck but he managed to gurgle, "Constable, do something!"

The other fellow with grain in the mill hollered, "Mebbe that galoot'll slip an fall outen the door!"

Everyone down on the ground uttered surly assents.

Louvin turned to them. "Git easy, the whole lot o yer! I'll be a-holden all o yer respons'ble if ennythin happens!"

A woman shouted behind them and they all flinched.

"Johnny!" It was Liza Dean. Jeb was there, too, arm around her waist.

Everyone turned to her then back to Johnny and Davy.

Johnny stopped and looked down at her. He let go of the noose around Davy's neck.

Davy thought this meant he had license to speak. "Mrs. Dean, tell this dolt I was not courting your daughter!"

Johnny grabbed the knot again.

Liza continued. "Let Mr. Davy go! He warnt intersted in Flora! Jes our lan'! That war jes his way o doin'!"

Johnny pulled in more slack. "Enuff fer me! Aint keered fer is atty-tude fum the git go!"

Someone in the crowd on the ground shouted, "True word!"

Davy dug his manicured fingernails into Johnny's hand at his neck and tried to back deeper into the building.

Johnny punched him in the stomach.

"Umph." As bending forward was a dangerous option, Davy buckled his knees and dropped to the floor. That took the remaining slack out of the rope. "Erck!"

Louvin yelled to the group on the ground, "Hole yore jaw!"

Liza screamed. "Stop it! Stop it all rat now! They's bin enuff killin! Enuff killin." She slid down, sat onto the ground and sobbed. "Enuff killin. ... Oh, my Flora! My dear Flora!" Now she was prostrate and sobbed into the sand. "Aaahahahahahah!"

Jeb struggled to get her to her feet. She was limp as a sack of corn meal. Once he did, he had to hold her up to withdraw from the scene.

Johnny let go of Davy. He left him at the doorway to struggle with the rope and his breath. He emerged from the mill and walked up to Louvin. "I air ready ter go, now."

"Awright, son." Louvin took him by an arm and began to walk him up the slope toward Charlie's.

Now outside, Davy complained from behind. "What about me, Constable Reilly! I'm hurt!"

Charlie called out. "'Pears ter me ter be fine, Luvin."

A few others agreed.

Davy continued. "He kidnapped and assaulted me!"

Louvin maintained his pace up the slope with Johnny. He did not even look back. "After what ye jes had ter say bout my friens, I air the wrong one ter complain ter."

Eli thought it was his turn. "What bout my store!?"

"Eli, after Johnny's trial, iffen ye don' like the re-sult, come talk ter me."

Louvin saw his horse at the hitching rail in front of Charlie's. He saw Jimmie perched on his barrel. Once he got within normal speaking range he asked, "Ye find Mizz Oxford?"

"She be on her way. 'Pears the ruckus air o'er."

"Yeah. Mizz Dean ended it fer everone." Louvin cocked his head. "Ye went ter the Dean's?"

"Figgered they oughter know."

"Ye air a good man, Jimmie Brown."

. . .

Inside the courtroom of the Claiborne County Courthouse in Tazewell, Tennessee, Louvin sat at the end of the prosecutor's table, squeezed between it and the jury box. Claiborne County Sheriff A.C. Hughes sat at the side. Lying on the table in front of him were the hickory stick and Louvin's envelope. A man in a business suit sat next to the Sheriff nearer the center of the room.

Jeb and Liza Dean sat in the pew directly behind that table.

Nellie Oxford sat alone in the pew directly behind the defense table. A man in a business suit sat at that table.

Johnny Oxford sat next to him, wearing his Sunday suit, manacles and a dejected look.

On the bench Judge Nelson Phelps looked up from examining the contents of a court file and toward the prosecutor's table. "Mr. Solicitor?"

The suit sitting there stood. "May it please the Court. Grainger Montgomery here for the State. Johnny Oxford is charged with first degree murder. He mercilessly beat his fiancée Flora Dean with a stick and threw her into the river by her home to drown. The State is ready for trial."

Phelps looked at the other table. "Johnny Oxford, how do you plead?"

Johnny and his lawyer stood. "May it please the Court. I am Patrick Fulkerson. I represent Mr. Oxford. Mr. Oxford wishes to plead guilty to second degree murder."

Judge Phelps looked at Solicitor Montgomery.

Montgomery looked at Jeb and Liza.

Jeb nodded.

Montgomery looked back at Judge Phelps. "The State is willing to accept that plea."

"Mr. Oxford, your lawyer says you wish to plead guilty to second degree murder. Is that true?"

Johnny wiped his face as best he could on his coat sleeve and took a deep breath. "Ye-es, Yer Honor."

Phelps resumed studying the contents of the folder for a while. He looked up at Johnny.

"These are pretty serious charges, son. You sure you want to plead? You have the right to make the State prove its case."

"Yessir."

"Anyone pressuring you to plead? Promising you anything? Like a light sentence, or parole?"

"Nawsir."

"Well then, why don't you tell me in your own words what happened?"

"Yessir. I, uh, I went ter Flora's on Sunday as usual. After supper we went a-walkin long the river by her place. She was talkin bout our weddin. Talkin an talkin. Fine'ly, I dun heerd enuff."

Johnny began to turn his head toward Jeb and Liza but couldn't follow through. He settled for staring at the feet of the court reporter seated in front of the bench. "I picked a stick up off the groun an hit her in the haid. She drapped ter the groun. She got up onter er knees. I member er sayin sumthin like, 'Oh Johnny dear, don' kill me here; I'm unprepared ter die.' I dint pay her no mind; I jes hit er sum more. Then, she was layin thar in the road real still like. I saw she was still breathin. I grabbed er by er har an drug er down the bank an threw er in ter the river. I watched er float on down outer sight. Then I went home."

Everyone in the entire courtroom was very still and very quiet for a very long time, all eyes on Johnny.

Except Jeb's and Liza's. Hers were covered by both her hands. All were pressed against Jeb's chest.

His stared at the front panel of the witness box. They manifested his will that Johnny's heart explode.

Phelps broke the spell. "That is the worst thing I have ever heard of! What could possibly cause you to do such a thing!?"

Johnny hung his head and began to sniffle. "I caint splain it. I luved er! Luved her more'n ennythin! Wanted ter merry er. But then she got all took up wit that thar Ainglish feller. I got powerful riled. All that talkin that night bout merryin. Ter my o thinkin she was makin a fool o me."

Phelps queried, "Ainglish feller? Who's that?"

Montgomery stood. "May it please the Court?"

"Yes, Mr. Montgomery?"

"This is Constable Louvin Reilly." He looked back at Louvin and gestured for him to stand. "He lives and patrols around Cumberland Gap for Sheriff Hughes. I believe he might know."

Phelps looked at Louvin. "Well?"

Louvin got up. "Ye, Ye-es, Yer Honor. He air re-ferrin ter Jack Davy, out er Middlesboro. Mr. Davy air buyin lan' roun the Gap fer is coal comp'ny. He was talkin mighty hard ter Mr. an Mizz Dean bout sellin thar lan'. It 'peared ter me like he was treatin Miss Flora extry spec'al on that 'count."

Phelps turned back to Johnny. "Could that be it, Johnny?

"Y, ye-es, Yer Honor. I r, reckon."

Johnny now addressed the table top in front of him. "Bin in truble all my life. Fightin. Drankin. Stealin. Paw war a mean drunk. Beat us chi'ren an Maw all the time. Beat Maw purty bad las time. I stepped in. Judge yander in Sneedvull tole me ter git outer is county. Come here ter werk fer Mr. Miler. Met Flora. Fust time in me life I felt like thangs war a-gittin better fer me. She made me feel good bout mesef."

Now he looked straight at Jeb and Liza. "Hepped me ter be a better person." He looked back at Phelps. "I got powerful skeered o losin all that. She war the bestes thang what ever happint ter me." He looked back at Jeb and Liza. "The bestes thang what ever happint ter me."

He sat and buried his face in his arms folded on the table.

Fulkerson sat back down and placed a hand on Johnny's shoulder.

His mother stood, stretched over the rail, placed her hands and head on her son's back and bawled.

Liza mashed her face deeper into Jeb's chest and sobbed likewise.

The rest of the crowd began to stir and murmur in sympathy.

Phelps gaveled his courtroom back to silence. "Order! Order! Yes, well now everybody has lost her. All right, you and Mr. Fulkerson stand up."

Johnny and Fulkerson obliged, Fulkerson helping Johnny up.

"It is the decision of this Court to find you, Johnny Oxford, guilty of murder in the second degree for killing Flora Dean and to sentence you to serve twenty years at hard labor in the state penitentiary. And it is so ordered!" With that the judge banged his gavel once more, stood up and departed.

The Bailiff called, "All rise!"

Everyone did as ordered.

Two guards appeared and ushered Johnny out.

The mommas, still sobbing, made to leave.

Jeb, looking helpless and profoundly awkward, bowed to Johnny's momma as she reached the aisle and allowed her to go ahead of him behind Liza.

The crowd streamed out the front door of the courthouse.

Having been further into the courtroom, Louvin was one of the last to exit. He looked around and found who he was looking for. He trotted over to Jeb and Liza, who were seated in their buckboard making ready to drive off. "Liza, agin, I air parful sorry bout Flora. Ye satisfied wit that thar judge's de-sciss'on?"

"I reckon; though nuthin air gonter bring my baby back."

"Naw'm. Reckon not. Ye goin home, now?"

Jeb finally spoke. "Aint feelin much like home no more. Reckon we'll sell ter Mr. Davy."

"Well now, I air shore sorry ter heer that. Ye built that farm outter nuthin. Flora was bornded thar. Whar will ye go?"

"Minded ter move south further down the Powell. We'll be awright. Mr. Davy dun made us a right genrous offer." Jeb flicked the reins. "Git up!"

Louvin watched the Deans leave for a moment. He walked over to his horse and mounted up. He reset his hat, rubbed the back of his neck and urged his horse up the road toward home and his own daughter.

3

Polly Vaughn

Polly Vaughn lived with her father's brother, Bill, and his wife, Peggy. She had lived with her aunt and uncle ever since her parents had died from small pox within an hour of each other six years ago. Her aunt and uncle were childless, and she was their only kin of that generation, so everything pointed to them as being the best guardians for Polly until she came of age. At sixteen she was ready to come of age. Really ready.

She now studied herself in the tall mirror which stood on its own floor stand in the sunniest spot of her corner of the cabin. She was only five-feet-tall, so she saw her entire body in the glass. She saw straight raven-black hair which ordinarily reached three fourths of the way down her back. Right now, though, she had it all pulled around over her left shoulder, covering her left breast.

She saw white skin all over. It was as white as the milk Aunt Peggy squeezed from her cows every morning. Polly sometimes hoped that the three dozen or so faint freckles scattered across the bridge of her nose and tops of her cheeks would disappear so that her skin would be flawless.

That reminded her of something. Over her shoulder she called, "Aunt Peggy!?"

"No call ter shout, dear; I air jes crosst the room."

"Did ye git them thar stains outter my apron?"

"Took a heap a bluin'; but, I blieve I got em all."

They called it an apron because they weren't sure how to pronounce the word "pelisse" that was printed on the pattern's package.

"That durned Jimmy Randall! Jumped right off his hoss inter that mud next to me!"

"Oh, I air a-thinkin twernt delibrate. He was jes happy ter see yer. Ye looked so purty; he wasn't lookin et the groun."

"S'pose so."

"Ye shore pitched a mighty fit, though. Right in front er all them folkses at Eli's store."

"I couldn hep it. Ye had werked an werked on that apron. Ye knew it come out purtier than ye had imagined. I was so proud er it, an o ye fer makin it fer me. I wanted ter wear it right then; show everbody what ye had dun with that thar bolt o plain white cloth Mr. Parch couldn sell. An walkin ter the settlement I was so careful ter keep it off the groun."

"I saw how ye fairly capered up ter his store wit yore nose in the air, showin off in front er all them other gals."

"Ye-es, an how they all cackled liked hens when Jimmy splashed me!"

"I wander if ye hurt is feelins."

"Oh, he air all right. Men don' pay no tention to us gals."

"Ye saw how red is face tarned. An ye saw how he looked at yer an th'other gals. An he said nary a word. Dint e'en say he was sorry. Jes got back up an rode on off. May be he air a-havin secon thoughts bout merryin yer."

"Stop it, Aunt Peggy! That air a turrble, mean thang ter say! He air fine! I heerd im pologize. We bin courtin long nough ter whar I knows what I kin ..., I mean what he will ..., oh jes lemme see my apron!"

A long, exhausting, fruitless day! The young man tramped through the underbrush of the woods by the millpond with no quarry. He cradled his double-barrel-muzzle-loading shotgun in his left arm and recounted all the missed shots of the day. As he really puzzled over that last rabbit, the overcast sky added injury to insult with a light drizzle. The trees broke that up into a heavy mist. "Fine! A cole, dark, wet, an empty-han-ed slog ter home!"

He reached the path leading to the settlement and turned in that direction. The sodden brim of his hat sagged to just below his eyes. He just caught a hint of white through the underbrush up the trail.

He stopped stock still. He raised his head as slowly as possible to get a better view. Something definitely out of place. White. And big. As he watched this thing he ever so slowly slid his right hand across his torso to the grip of his shotgun. Equally as slowly he drew the butt out from under his arm and cocked both hammers. He never remembered the clicks being so loud.

He side stepped to behind a tree and took a deep breath. He peered around to watch this thing. It lay hard against the trunk of a small bushy tree. It did not move. The young man decided it was some kind of animal seeking shelter from the heavy mist swirling around under the canopy of these woods. He needed a closer look and a better angle from which to shoot. "Durn if I miss thisn."

Eyes always on his prey he trod heel to toe to behind a closer tree. He repeated this maneuver two more times before being sure he had a clear shot within killing range. He studied the thing from behind this last tree. He needed to know what it was. It could be someone's lost calf. He saw it finally move. He saw a streak of jet black. *A swan from the mill pond*, he realized. "Ole Man Miler aint gonter miss one." He raised his gun to his shoulder and aimed. He squeezed the back trigger. PaBOOM!

The white thing jerked, screamed in a woman's voice, and lay still.

The young man completely let go of his gun and stood motionless in the cloud of smoke and water vapor. The coldness that sprang up inside his body surpassed that which bedeviled him from outside. He willed his legs to move, but they took a moment to respond. Finally he was sprinting.

He knelt beside a bundle of white cloth. Spots of blood spread away from holes in the damp fabric. The toe of a tiny black boot stuck out from one end, helping the boy figure out where to search for a head. He unwrapped more white cloth away from the face of Polly Vaughn.

"Polly!"

That iciness he had felt inside him earlier now seized every muscle and organ. It paralyzed his brain. His vision blurred.

"Polly! Oh, Polly, I seed ye ez a swan!" He began to cry. "Oh Polly, I air sorry! Parful sorry! Please don' die! I'll take ye home rat now. Hole on, dear! Oh, Oh, Oh!"

The familiar voice roused Polly a bit. She smiled. Jimmy had come to save her. She felt herself rising up off the ground. Now strong arms cradled her against a warm torso.

Jimmy was sprinting again. As best he could while trying to be careful with a gravely injured fiancée in his arms.

The rain fell harder.

Outside a large log barn the rain poured down. The barn's big door was open. Lamp light and the muffled voices of two men emanated from inside.

Jimmy carried Polly straight in. Both were soaked. Jimmy laid Polly down on a pile of hay just inside.

The two men deeper inside turned and looked up to see what was going on.

The older one dropped the harness, needle and leather thong he was holding and ran over to Polly and Jimmy. "What happint; what happint? Oh, Polly!"

"I air sorry Mr. Vaughn. I was out huntin. It was a-rainin an gittin dark. She was all wrop-ped up in this hyar apron. She 'peared ter me ter be a swan. Hit war a axdent."

Bill Vaughn dropped to his knees beside Polly. He placed a palm on her cheek, took up one of her hands with his two and felt for a pulse at her wrist. He felt her neck. He bent down with an ear close to her nose, then jumped up. "She air daid! Jimmy, ye kilt er! Ye murdered my Polly, ye damned cussed basterd!"

Vaughn lunged at Jimmy and knocked him flat on his back, sliding him a foot or two across the hard packed ground. While straddling him he pummeled Jimmy's face and chest.

Jimmy raised his hands in defense but did not try to hit back. His defense was half-hearted; his grief and bewilderment annihilated all strength. He gasped, "Twere a axdent, a axdent I tell ye! I dint mean ter! I'd ne'er hurt her fer the wurl. I luv her!"

"Joe, git sum rope. We'll tie this no count varmint up an carry im ter Luvin termorry mornin. Rat now, I gots ter see ter Polly."

Joe came up with a couple of coils and both trussed Jimmy up to the point where he looked like a bug half wrapped in spider silk.

Vaughn enveloped Polly in her apron, picked her up and exited the barn.

Joe looked at Jimmy and then out at the rain. He finally exited, leaving Jimmy on the floor crying.

Well into the night Jimmy regained some composure and a practical mindset. "They'll hang me." All his strength returned. He rolled, writhed and kicked until the rope had stretched enough for him to wriggle out. He too exited the barn and headed for home.

Outside his cabin Jimmy could see the light of a healthy fire through a window. "Paw air still up a-waitin fer me." He stood there a while watching the warm light. He had to sort out many thoughts swirling through his mind. Finally, "Gots ter go on in an tell im g'bye fer ever." Jimmy entered and found his father sitting in a rocker, nudging lumps of coal in the fireplace with a poker. "I ... um. I air home."

Jimmy's father turned and the sight he saw compelled him out of his chair. He saw Jimmy's clothes thoroughly soaked and covered with mud, face and hands colorless. He rushed over to his forlorn son. "What happint!?"

The very warm air in the cabin began to thaw Jimmy out. His muscles began to relax after hours of tenseness against the weather and turmoil. All the horror of the day overcame him. His legs gave way. He sat hard on the floor and wept. "I kilt er! I kilt my Polly!"

The old man didn't know what to do, or say. He stood there looking down at his boy nonplussed. Then he eased down onto the floor next to Jimmy and put his arm around him.

Almost at the same time Jimmy jumped up onto his feet leaving his baffled father sitting there. "I gots ter go!" He rushed over to the cedar chest at the foot of his cot, opened it and started pulling out clothes and tossing them onto his bed. "Bill Vaughn air on my trail by now fer shore! I gots ter light outter here." He whirled around looking for anything he could stuff his clothes into. He settled upon a couple of burlap bags draped over a rafter. He pulled them down and began to cram in clothes. His father's hand on his shoulder scared the daylights out of him. He whirled around. "They air gonter hang me! I gots ter go! I caint ever come back! Sorry ter leave yer like this, Paw."

Frank Randall decided he needed to shout to get Jimmy to focus. "Stop! Rat now! Set down hyar an tell me what happint!"

That seemed to help. Jimmy immediately sat on his cot. Frank sat beside him and listened to Jimmy's tale. Once done, Jimmy was a lot calmer. He noticed the damp clothes he was wearing. He stripped down to his union suit and wrapped himself in the quilt that was at the foot of his cot. "An that air why I gots ter leave here and never come back."

"Ye aint goin nowhar. Iffen what ye air a-sayin air true, twere a axdent. They aint gonter hang ye fer that. Ye may have ter spen sum time in jail, sorry ter say; but they aint gonter hang ye. But, ye gots ter turn yesef in ter Luvin. Ye gots ter go now, afore Bill Vaughn cotches up wit ye an lynches yer hissef."

Jimmy began getting agitated again.

Frank put his arm around him. "I'll go wit yer. Come on. Put on sum dry clothes. Sum warm ones. Aint shore whar all ye will be fer a spell."

Jimmy blanched.

. . .

Claiborne County Sheriff A. C. Hughes appointed local people throughout the County as part time law enforcement officials to patrol areas around where they lived and attend to routine and more or less safe tasks such as serving papers and arresting folks for misdemeanors tried in the Justice of the Peace's court.

Constable Louvin Reilly was one such appointee who lived in the northwest region of the County near Cumberland Gap. He had no office to speak of. He had a stand up desk in the corner of Charlie Waggoner's blacksmith shop across the road from Eli Parch's Mercantile.

This morning Louvin leaned back against his desk as a man dressed in the clothes of industrial middle management paced back and forth and complained about too many of his miners coming to work hung over.

A commotion outside the front door of the shop interrupted the conversation. Bill Vaughn, his helper Joe, Jimmy and Frank Randall staggered through entangled and wrestling each other.

Louvin took a couple of steps toward them to place himself between the little mob and the mine manager. "What air all this bout?"

"Jimmy kilt Polly!" Bill shouted.

"Twere a axdent! Jimmy says it were a axdent." Frank rejoined.

"What!?" Louvin asked.

"Las night! He shot er!" Vaughn replied.

Louvin looked at Jimmy. Jimmy began to say something, but Louvin held up his hand to stop him. "Don' say a word!" He addressed the mine manager. "Why don' ye git on back ter yore werk. We kin jow more bout this later."

The mine manager gave Louvin a stern look and left.

Louvin turned to Bill. "What happint?"

"Las night me'n Joe was in my barn when this dad-burned no count varmint comes in a-carryin Polly an sayin he hed shot er. When I lookt to er she was daid!"

Louvin looked at Joe, who nodded in assent. He looked at Jimmy who just looked at the floor. He said, "Sorry Jimmy. I air bound ter chain ye ter that thar ring whilst I think on this." He pulled a pair of shackles out of the bottom drawer of his desk, took Jimmy by the arm and led him to a big iron ring spiked to the wall beyond his desk. He pointed to the mound of old blankets on the ground beneath it and Jimmy sat. Louvin locked one shackle on Jimmy's right wrist, led the chain through the ring and shackled Jimmy's left wrist.

He turned back to the others. "Bill, kin ye write?" Bill sort of nodded and shook his head at the same time. Louvin went back over to his desk. "Well, tell me everthink what happint. I'll write. How bout you-uns Frank?"

Frank was more forthright. "Naw."

"I'll take yore statement after Bill." Louvin retrieved paper, pen, and ink bottle from the top drawer of his desk, spread them all out on the desk top and set up to write. "Awright, Bill, les have it."

After both men had spoken, and Louvin had written, and they had made their marks on their statements, Louvin spoke. "This air shore de-sturbin bout Polly, Bill. I air truly sorrowful. Whar air she now?"

"Outside in my wagon."

"Outside!? Laws a mercy; why dint yer say so arlier? Can ye drive her ter Cummerlin Gap? I need fer Doc Massey ter make a report. I'll go long wit yer."

Bill nodded. Then he wrapped both his arms around himself, went over and leaned against Louvin's desk, face to the wall.

To Frank and Jimmy Louvin said, "You-uns unnerstan this deal air parful ser'ous. I gots ter take Jimmy ter the jailhouse in Tazewell. We'll set out soons I git back from Cummerlin."

Frank and Jimmy nodded. Frank went over and sat down on the ground next to Jimmy.

Louvin continued. "Jes stay here a minit. I gots ter tell Matt an Mark where I air a-goin."

Everyone nodded.

Louvin headed for the door. As he reached it he nearly ran into a statuesque, fortyish woman who was about to enter carrying a hat box. "Angeline! What air ye doin here!?"

Angeline half held out the box. "I. I baked ye a cake."

"A cake? Why'd ye go an do that fer?"

Angeline's bright eyes dimmed. "I. I like ter bake. I wanted ter bake sumthin fer ye."

Louvin closed his eyes and took a breath. He rubbed the back of his neck. "I air sorry, Angeline. That was rude. I was werkin sumthin out in my brain. Thank ee. Thank ee kindly. I know ye air a mighty fine baker. This means a lot ter me."

Angeline's eyes brightened back up a bit. She handed Louvin the box.

He took it and looked around wondering what to do with it under all the circumstances.

"If thars anythin I kin e'er do fer ye, Luvin, jes lemme know."

"Er, thank ee, Angeline. ... Know what? Ye kin hep me rat now. Come in hyar an set with Bill Vaughn and Frank and Jimmy Randall. Share some o this cake wit em. I'll be back directly."

Angeline's eyes resumed their original brilliance. "Course, Luvin. My pleasure."

Louvin handed her the box back and stepped aside to allow her to enter. He exited the shop.

Angeline stepped in. "'lo, Bill, Frank. What's brung all a yer ter the settlemint ter day? Jimmy!"

. . .

Jimmy slept soundly on the cot in his jail cell. Bill Vaughn had not killed him. His father believed in him. Louvin was not judgmental at all. Angeline had brought him hot food and one of her famous cakes before he had left the settlement. He was warm and dry.

A quiet female voice called out from nowhere. "Jimmy. . . . Jimmy."

Jimmy jerked awake. "Eh? What?" He looked around into the cellblock, but saw no one. He settled back down.

A few minutes passed.

Now an apparition began to form in the cell next to Jimmy's. "Jimmy."

Jimmy stirred again and sat up turning toward the corridor along the front of the cells. "What, dangit!? Who be thar!?" Jimmy moved from cot to cell door. He saw no one in the corridor so turned back around. He saw Polly. She was wearing the white apron. She was whole and beautiful, glowing and translucent. "AAAH!"

Polly floated to the side of his cell. She grasped bars with her hands and situated her face between them. "Don' be skeerd, Jimmy. I air gonter hep ye. I know ye dint mean ter kill me. Twere a axdent. I set down under that thar tree ter wait out the rain. I had this apron wropp-ed roun me. Ye took me fer one o them thar swans fum the millpond. Jes keep tellin everbody that. Ye hear, Jimmy? Keep tellin everbody that. E'en to yore trial. They'll believe ye. I swar. Promise me, Jimmy, ye'll keep tellin em that. Ye do and ye'll be awright."

Jimmy just stood at the cell door, arms limp by his sides, staring at his beloved. "Uh, huh . . . Yeah . . . Okay."

Polly floated away from Jimmy's cell, clasped her hands together below her chin and began to fade. "Give me yore word."

"I . . . My word."

Polly blew a kiss and disappeared.

It was dark in the cell block again.

Jimmy sat down on the edge of his cot, elbows on knees and face in hands. He took a deep breath and blew it out.

. . .

The court room in the Claiborne County Courthouse in Tazewell, Tennessee was laid out with a main entrance in the center of the back wall and an aisle leading from the entrance, between banks of pews, to swinging gates hinged in the center of a rail separating the pews from the work area of the room. Two counsel tables were directly on the other side of the rail. Just beyond them was the jury box against the right side wall by the prosecutor's table. The judge's bench and witness box were in the center of the wall opposite the main entrance, with the witness box on the side nearer the jury. On each side of that unit were doors in the wall.

A small table sat against the front of the judge's bench. Stacks of paper, ink bottles, fountain pens and a pile of folders lay on the table.

A man wearing a suit and string tie sat there polishing a pen with a cloth. He squinted through what in the future would be called coke bottle glasses.

Twelve men sat in the jury box. Assorted people dressed in their Sunday clothes milled around the spectator area of the courtroom. Some sat in the pews. Some stood along the back and sides. Many of both groups chatted together quietly.

Louvin Reilly, in his Sunday suit, sat alone at one end of the prosecutor's table, squeezed between it and the jury box. Bill and Peggy Vaughn sat in the pew directly behind that table. Frank Randall sat alone in the pew directly behind the defense table. None of these people interacted with anyone. Bill and Frank had not even looked at each other since arriving.

Three men entered the courtroom together through the main entrance. Two were dressed in business suits. The other was in a basic law enforcement uniform. The two suits carried brief cases. The uniform carried a parcel loosely wrapped in craft paper. As the three walked up the aisle they conversed with each other very congenially. As they reached the swinging gates they stopped talking. As they passed through the gates they split.

One suit plopped his belongings onto the prosecutor's table and plopped his behind in a chair. The uniform sat between him and Louvin and set his parcel on the table. They each shook Louvin's hand and all three talked quietly, referring to some handwritten documents the suit pulled from his case.

The other suit set up at the defense table, turned and greeted Frank Randall over the rail.

A young man in a uniform similar to the one worn by the fellow that had just come in entered the courtroom through the door in the back wall opposite the bench from the witness box. "Hear ye, hear ye! Court air in sess'on! Honor'ble Nelson Phelps presidin! All rise!"

Everyone in the courtroom stopped whatever they were doing and faced the bench. Those seated stood.

A middle aged man dressed in a judicial robe entered the courtroom through the same back door and mounted the bench. He stood there and surveyed the crowd. He appeared pleased with the turnout. "Thank you all. Please be seated. Bailiff, call the next case." The judge and everyone else sat.

The young uniformed man went to the table in front of the bench and picked up the folder on the top of the pile. He looked at its tab and called out. "State er Tennessee agin Jimmy Randall!" He handed the folder up to Judge Phelps.

Two guards entered through the back door escorting Jimmy Randall to his seat at the defense table. Jimmy was dressed in his Sunday best and manacles. He was calm, but looked a little worried.

His father stood and held out his right hand. Jimmy took it in both of his.

"Gots a good holt er the faith, Jimmy?"

"Yessir, Paw. Blieve so."

Both took their respective seats.

The judge pored over the folder. He looked up at the prosecutor's table. "Mr. Montgomery?"

The court reporter took to his task.

The Solicitor stood. "May it please the Court, Grainger Montgomery here for the State. Jimmy Randall is charged with first degree murder. He shot his fiancée Polly Vaughn to death. The State is ready to proceed."

Judge Phelps looked over at the defense table. "Mr. Randall, how do you plead?"

Jimmy and his lawyer rose. "May it please the Court. I am Patrick Fulkerson. I represent Mr. Randall. Mr. Randall wishes to plead ...."

Jimmy finished the plea, "Haint guilty, Yer Honor!"

Fulkerson looked at Jimmy, grabbed his arm and looked back at the judge. "Beggin the Court's indulgence, Judge. May I speak with my client?"

"Looks like that might be appropriate. But, make it quick." Phelps watched Fulkerson sit and drag Jimmy down into his own seat. He saw the two lean in and talk in voices too low for him to hear. He noticed some of the crowd lean in to try. He saw Fulkerson pull hand-written documents out of his briefcase and wave them at Jimmy. He saw Frank Randall lean in and join the conversation. He noticed Mr. Randall looked puzzled. He watched Jimmy just keep wagging his head.

Finally Fulkerson leaned away, flicked his eyes upward and stood. He looked down at Jimmy, who took the cue and stood. "Sorry, yer Honor. Mr. Randall is stubborn, er, steadfast in his plea."

"All right, Mr. Randall, I ask again, guilty or not?"

"Not, Yer Honor."

"Very well. Mr. Montgomery, call your first witness."

"Thank you, Your Honor. The State calls William Vaughn to the stand."

Bill sprang up and marched to the witness box. There he met the bailiff who had a book with a faded black cover in his left hand.

The bailiff raised that waist high and raised his right hand just as high as he could. "Place yore lef han on this hyar Bible an raise yore right."

Vaughn did as directed.

"Do ye solemnly swar ter tell the truth, th'ole truth an nuthin but the truth, so hep ye God?"

"I do!"

The bailiff pointed to the witness box. "Sit thar."

Again Vaughn did as directed.

Montgomery moved from his spot at his table to a spot right in front of the jury box, facing Bill. "All right, Mr. Vaughn. Tell us your full name and where you live, for the record."

"Eh. William Vaughn. Live a-nigh Cummerlin Gap."

"How did you know the victim of this most tragic crime?"

"Polly was my niece. Bin livin with us oh, nigh onter six yar, since my bruther an is wife up an died o the small pox."

"Very good, Mr. Vaughn. You're doing fine. Now tell us in your own words what you saw and did that dreadful night; and I apologize for having to bring up such painful memories; but it is necessary."

"Uh, shore. Eh. Me'n my hep. Joe Clark? Was in my barn mendin a harness when Jimmy come in out the rain a-carryin Polly. Both were soakin wet. She was all limp. He laid her down on sum hay an said he'd shot er. I come o'er an looked at er, an, AN SHE WAS DAID!" Bill leaned forward and stood part way up from the chair, hands on the armrests.

Despite Bill's histrionics a few spectators diverted their attention from him to a bright spot developing on the floor between the defense table and the bench. They pointed and whispered to each other.

Judge Phelps noticed and raised his gavel.

Montgomery continued. "Now, again, Mr. Vaughn, I am truly sorry to have to ask these most sensitive questions, but please try to maintain your composure, out of respect for these proceedings. Then what happened?"

"I kinder los my haid. I took ter layin onter Jimmy hard as I could. Then I tied ...."

Now jurors turned from Vaughn to the floor.

A large, misty, white ovoid was forming in the bright spot.

Vaughn followed their gaze.

The egg began to solidify.

"Then what, Mr. Vaughn?"

Seeing everyone's attention sidetracked, Phelps banged his gavel. "Order! Mr. Vaughn, answer the question!"

"Uh. Yessir. I was sayin, I tied Jimmy up." He was still looking at the egg.

It assumed the details of a swan with its head tucked under its wing.

Montgomery kept trying to recapture Vaughn's attention. "And then what? Mr. Vaughn?"

The swan's head emerged from its wing and stretched upward.

Vaughn looked back at Montgomery. "I picked Polly up off the floor."

The swan's neck stretched upward more than the usual swan's neck. As it did it thickened and the swan's body diminished.

Vaughn looked back at this process.

Montgomery continued in a little louder voice. "You picked Polly up and did what, Mr. Vaughn?"

The transformation ended; the swan was now the form of a diminutive woman.

Everyone but Judge Phelps stood up.

Vaughn cried, "Polly! Polly!"

Polly Vaughn was as whole, white and radiant as she was when she appeared to Jimmy that night in the jailhouse.

Phelps appeared resolved to hold somebody in contempt. "Who the …? Bailiff, take charge of that woman! Everybody sit back down!"

The bailiff remained fixed at his station.

Everyone remained standing.

Louvin cried, "Polly Vaughn! Yer Honor, that air Polly Vaughn! The gal what got shot!"

Phelps was irritated his staff was balking. "Bailiff!"

The bailiff cut his eyes from Polly to Phelps but otherwise remained motionless.

Spectators and jurors jabbered amongst themselves and pointed at Polly.

Montgomery yelled. "Mistrial! Mistrial! This woman is disrupting my case!"

Judge Phelps stood up, staring at Polly. "ORDER! BAILIFF!"

Polly raised her hand and everyone fell silent.

She floated over to her uncle. She passed Montgomery, who backed himself against the jury box.

"Jimmy air innercent, Uncle Bill! Twere a axdent. I was walkin that path along o the mill pond near dark. It took ter rainin. I pulled this apron roun me an sot under a tree ter wait it out. Jimmy took me fer a swan from the millpond!" She looked up at Phelps, who was looking down at her with his mouth open. "Let im go, yer Honor. Please let im go. I know he luvs me an would ne'er hurt me on purpose!"

Polly glided over to Jimmy.

"Polly." Jimmy reached for her, but his hands passed through her outstretched hands. They smiled at each other. "I luv ye, Polly."

"I luv ye, Jimmy. G'bye." Polly returned to where she had originated and began to dissolve.

Blowing him a kiss was the last discernible thing anyone saw.

The spot on the floor still glowed.

"G'bye, Polly. I luv ye, too. I air so sorry. So, so sorry." Jimmy sat back down, folded his arms on the table, rested his face on them and quietly wept.

Everyone stirred again and began chattering with each other.

Phelps came back around and started banging the heck out of his bench with his gavel. "Order! ... Order! ... ORDER, goll durn it!"

Everyone settled and sat down.

Phelps closed his eyes and took a deep breath. He turned to Montgomery, who was hard against the jury box staring at the bright spot on the floor. "What do you want to do, Mr. Montgomery?"

Montgomery failed to respond.

"MONTY!"

Montgomery flinched. "Uh, sorry, your Honor." He looked at Vaughn, inviting comment.

Vaughn looked down at his knees. "I, I reckon I'll drap the charges."

"You sure?" Montgomery asked.

Vaughn looked up and over at Peggy.

She had a hanky at her nose. She nodded.

Vaughn said, "Yeah. Awright. I'll accept it twere a axdent." He looked back at his knees. "My precious Polly."

Montgomery put his hands on his hips. "Huh! Well, if that's what Mr. and Mizz Vaughn want, the State will have to agree."

Phelps proclaimed, "Very well then! I hereby rule Polly Vaughn's death to be accidental! Case dismissed!" He rapped his gavel once again, jumped up and swiftly headed for his door.

The bailiff finally moved, to open the door for Phelps. "All rise!" Everyone obeyed.

Phelps exited with the bailiff disrespectfully close behind.

The totally professional court reporter finished writing Phelps' last words before tossing his pen down and leaving, too.

Decorum in the courtroom degenerated. Everyone broke into boisterous talking and gesturing.

A guard came out and unshackled Jimmy.

Fulkerson took Jimmy's now free right hand in both of his, smiled and stammered out amazed congratulations and queries.

Frank Randall stepped right over the rail and hugged them both.

During all this Solicitor Montgomery picked up the parcel wrapped in craft paper off his table. He pulled the craft paper away from Polly's neatly folded apron. Some of its folds showed dark reddish brown stains. Montgomery passed through the swinging gates, bowed a little and offered it to Peggy.

She took and hugged it.

4

The Johnson Boys

Matthew and Mark Johnson together carried a large sack labeled sugar from inside the storeroom at the back of Eli Parch's Mercantile and heaved it up into a teamster's wagon. They climbed in, dragged the sack forward and lifted it onto a similar sack. They took a moment to appreciate the community's return to normalcy.

At the same time two girls rounded the corner from the front of the store. Both wore cotton print dresses and complimentary kerchiefs, shawls and bonnets. One was a tall, fair skinned blonde with blue eyes. The other was a shorter brunette with brown eyes and tanned complexion. Both were prettier than the boys were handsome.

The blonde said, "'lo, Matt."

The brunette said, "Hi, Mark."

The boys stopped, straightened up, looked at the girls, then looked at each other. Matt looked back at the girls, but Mark jumped off the back of the wagon.

Matt said, "Uuh. Errr. Lo, Cindy; Katy."

Matt followed Mark off the back of the wagon to two stout boards leaning against the wall of the storeroom. Each boy took one and they set them as ramps at the back end of the wagon. They took some time adjusting them and stamping on the ends on the ground, ignoring the girls.

Cindy, the blonde, said, "Parful rain las night. Lef these roads a mess."

"Uh, huh." Both boys entered the storeroom.

Both girls remained outside beside the wagon.

A minute passed.

Then both boys emerged rolling a barrel labeled molasses.

Cindy tried again. "Matt, that thar apple tree by yore cabin got enny apples this yar?"

"Um. Sum, I reckon." The boys began rolling the barrel up the boards.

"May I come by someday soon an git sum? I'll bake ye a pie."

"Eh. Shore. Git all ye air a-minded ter." The boys continued to push the barrel up the boards.

Katy the brunette tried. "Say, Mark. That yore hat back thar on the porch? Th'one a-sportin that big claw?"

"What? Oh. Uh. Yeh." The boys got the barrel to the bed of the wagon. They stopped for a short breather, looking more at the sky and the walls of the storeroom than at the girls. They climbed into the back of the wagon, rolled the barrel toward the front, turned it upright and scooted it close to the sacks of sugar.

"I heerd ye boys kilt a bar." Katy tried to sound only mildly interested.

"A while back." The boys jumped off the wagon and entered the storeroom.

The girls moved closer to the door of the storeroom and waited.

The boys rolled out another barrel marked molasses.

"Still, yer muster bin skeered." Cindy said.

"Bout what?" Mark asked.

"Th' bar!" Both girls shouted together.

"Oh. Yeah. Nuthin ter talk bout." The boys positioned the barrel at the bottom of the ramp. "Ole Rattler dun mos' th' werk." The boys began pushing that barrel up.

Cindy experimented with another tack. She took her bonnet off. "Ew, shore air steamy after that rain las night! Settin on the mill dam with my feet in that cool water would be nice. What air ye boys a-thinkin?"

Katy liked that tack. She pulled her bonnet off and raked her fingers upward through her hair on the back of her head lifting it off her neck. "Oh, ye-es!"

With the second barrel about halfway up the ramp, Matt said, "I air a-thinkin ye bes take keer not ter rile ole man Miler. Th' board on this side air a-slippin! Let er back down, Mark. Hurry!"

As quickly as they could without losing control of it the boys rolled the barrel back down the ramp.

Matt's board slipped off the wagon.

The barrel tipped in his direction. Its edge hit the ground and the whole thing bounced.

The boys kept all hands on the barrel to control it. As they did they backed extra close alongside the storeroom door.

Mark brushed against a hinge, which snagged a pants pocket of his overalls and ripped a huge hole that revealed a whole lot of leg skin. The boys stopped at the sound of ripping denim.

Mark looked down. His blush made his freckles all but disappear. "Dangit!"

Both girls brought their bonnets up against their faces, looked at each other and struggled hard to repress giggles.

Katy regained composure first. "I can mend them thar jeans fer yer, Mark."

"No thank ee! I bin mendin my own clothes ever since … fer yars!" He experimented with numbers of ways to hold his pants together with both hands.

Matt advised, "Mr. Parch has needle an thread in is store."

Both boys disappeared into the storeroom. Mark walked stooped over holding his pants leg closed.

Cindy stomped up to the door but did not enter. "I declar ter th' mercy seat ye Johnson boys beat all I ever seen! Ye unnerstan? Beat all I ever seen! Come on, Katy!"

They turned and nearly collided with Matt and Mark's uncle Constable Louvin Reilly.

"'lo, gals. Matt an Mark in thar?"

"'lo, Mr. Reilly. Yessir."

The boys emerged from the storeroom. Mark was still stooped over holding his pants together.

The girls hopped from dry spot to dry spot back around the corner of the store.

Louvin said, "I gots ter go ter the Gap an then right straight yander ter Tazewell. That'll keep me way fum here till termorry evenin. Jes in case ennybody axes."

"Yessir."

"Cindy and Katy, eh? They's good gals. An o course, mighty purty. They'd make fine mates."

"Aw, Uncle Luvin, don' start that talkin agin."

"Look a-here. Ye dun bin on yer own fer too long. High time ter be thinkin serous bout settlin down an raisin a famly. Mark, ye could start by axin Katy ter mend yore pants." Louvin left and picked his way back across the muddy road leaving Matt and Mark watching him depart.

The flames of a cozy fire of burning coal in a stone fireplace danced to the tune of "Haste To The Wedding" being played by a fiddle accompanied by a claw hammer banjo. Fire and music warmed the interior of a single pen log cabin.

Matt and Mark sat in ladder-back chairs to one side of the fire. Matt played the fiddle and Mark played the open-back banjo. They were entertaining Louvin and his daughter Lucy Lee, also sitting in ladder-back chairs on the other side of the fireplace. After three rounds the boys finished and Louvin and Lucy Lee clapped.

"That was wonderful!"

"Thank ee, Lucy."

"I want yer ter play at my weddin."

"Shore, cuz. Goes thout sayin." Matt said.

"Enny stew lef?" Mark inquired.

"Look in that pot on the hearth." Lucy offered.

Mark leaned over from his chair, took the lid off the Dutch oven and peered inside. "Naw. All gone. Twas bo-dac'ous."

"Thank ee. An thank ee fer the squirrels. An I know Paw air obleeged fer yore hep of late, too."

"That air true. Hit air mighty greeable ter hev two good men I can count on roun here. Couldna got crosst that river an back thout ye."

"All thas a-happnin roun here of late air keepin me awake at night. I air tuckered out," Mark yawned.

"Same here," Matt rolled his shoulders and stretched.

Louvin started in. "Ye boys. Bin fendin fer yerseves twelve yar an better. Bin huntin, fishin, an trappin all yore lives. After that far, ye built back yore mam an pap's cabin when ye was jes chillen. Ye an Rattler even took Ole Slew Foot. I figgered ye'd have a better grip on all this."

Matt picked a loose hair off his bow.

Mark adjusted the tuning on his banjo.

Lucy interceded, "Paw! Go easy on em. . Happnins roun here air tryin everbody!"

"Aah, I know yer right. Sorry. Seen two young-uns kilt an one carried off ter prison. Had ter tell two mommas they'd los thar babies. Had ter toughen up my mine fer all that. Reckon I aint turned it loose, yit, either. . . . Oh. Say, Lucy, ye oughter seen how Cindy Grove an Katy Daly were be-havin roun Matt n Mark Sattidy."

"That so?" Lucy looked over at them.

They looked more intently at their instruments.

Louvin continued. "Yes sir! Saw em at Eli's store. They seemed parful intersted in em. Aint that right, Mark?"

"I, I reckon. We was busy loadin that thar wagon fer Mr. Parch. Wasn't payin much mind."

"Well, ye bes be startin. They both air good gals."

Matt said to Mark, "Katy shore studied up on that rip in yore overhauls."

"Hole yore jaw!"

Matt laughed and Mark frowned.

Louvin interceded. "Git easy. Point is, ye boys gots ter be gittin ser'ous bout settlin down an makin sumthin o yerseves. Git on outer these mountins. Go ter Knoxvull. Yer smart an strong. Ye can do ennythin y'air a-minded ter, an be durn good at it. Ye larned them thar insterments an them thar poems. Yer awready doin what Parson Brown bin preachin bout. Ye'd fair very well fer yerseves an yore famlies."

"I air doin what I want." Matt protested.

"As am I!" Mark added.

"What air Jack Davy sayin bout yore mountin?"

Things got quiet. The boys found more things on their instruments to attend to.

As Mark checked the tailpiece on his banjo he said, "He 'lows ez it air migh nigh solit coal."

Louvin whistled. "He made yer an offer?"

"Sevral," Matt said.

"They fair?"

"I air thinkin that las offer was mor'n fair." Matt said. As he spoke he looked at Mark.

Mark nodded.

"What air ye waitin fer?"

"That mountin air our home."

"Ye oughter be lookin hard at Mr. Davy's offer. Oughter be lookin ter yore future. I know ye could git nough ter move ter town an learn a trade, e'en a perfess'on. Ye could make a real good livin. Time air a-wastin."

"Mark an me dun studied on it. 'Pears ter me we'd be losin our freedom." Matt said.

Louvin returned. "Yore ways o doin can git mighty lonely. Ye bin studyin on female compan'onship, too, aint ye?"

Matt pulled his fiddle's case lying on the floor toward him and laid his instrument and bow in place.

Mark picked up a burlap bag from the floor and slid his banjo into it.

While bent over tending to his instrument Matt said, "I reckon. Jes aint feelin it, yit."

Louvin continued. "Ye boys air migh nigh 23 an 25 yar old. Mos' men yore age gots chillen o thar own, now."

"Still plenty o time fer us."

"I saw how ye war roun them gals. Ye coulder quit werkin fer one minit jes ter talk wit em."

"Aw, Uncle Luvin."

"Serous. This shyness roun wimmin has got ter quit."

"I gots ter agree wit Paw, thar. Jes think of em as enny other person. S'all thar is ter it." Lucy joined.

Both boys stood up from their chairs with their instruments.

Rattler stood up from where he had been lying in the corner.

Matt declared, "I dun heerd enuff! We air fine! Leave us be!"

Mark joined, "Ye go on bout this constantly. I air gittin shet o this."

Both headed for the door and Rattler followed.

Matt turned to Lucy. "Lucy, thank ee agin fer supper. This air the las time I'll be a-comin here. Ye might not see me fer a long spell."

"Same here!"

Lucy and Louvin stood up.

"Don' say that!" Lucy objected.

"Boys! Thems mighty hard words!"

"Don' keer!"

"G'bye!"

Both reached the door. Matt opened it, Rattler slipped out and Matt exited. Mark followed and slammed the door shut.

Louvin and Lucy watched the door a moment prepared for it to open again. Then they looked at each other.

"They aint serous. Air they?" Lucy asked.

"Ida know. They air the stubbornest people I ever met."

Lucy sighed, shrugged her shoulders, went over to the fireplace and picked up the Dutch oven.

Louvin rubbed the back of his neck and continued to watch the door.

. . .

A grassy meadow swept up from a little river to a tree line. An outcropping of rocks accessorized the tree line.

A short distance away a dog bayed.

A Plott Hound appeared, continuing to bay, nose down, running along the tree line. It reached the outcropping and began furiously scratching at a spot, still baying his head off.

Matt and Mark trotted up to the dog, a tad out of breath. Matt carried a well-used Model 1861 Springfield. Slung over Mark's shoulder was an equally worn tarred canvas haversack. The rip in his pants had been expertly mended. Both had left their visit with Uncle Louvin and Cousin Lucy a few days ago well behind them.

Mark grabbed the dog's thick neck and struggled to pull him away from a burrow. "Whistlepig! ... Rattler caint dig through these here rocks."

"Need us a pole." Matt advised.

"I'll tie Rattler up an cut a saplin."

Matt climbed up to the top of the pile of rocks and sat down with the rifle across his lap. "I'll set here an watch if he comes out."

Mark pulled a piece of rope out of his sack and tied it around Rattler's neck. He tugged Rattler toward the woods, which was difficult because Rattler was reluctant to leave his quarry. "Here, dawg!" He tied his dog to a tree at woods edge and disappeared into the woods.

Matt bided his time watching tree tops, clouds, and a pair of eagles soaring over the river.

"The hills in the Highlan's air bonnie,
Wi' the light an the shadder at play;
An the win's that make redder the heather
Fer up on the cliff an the bray.
    The white clouds air floatin above em,
Like snowdrif's that ne'er can faw,
The hills in the Highlan's air bonnie,
The hills in the Highlan's air braw."

"What air takin ser long?"

From the woods Mark replied, "Barlow's gittin dull."

"Tole yer ter bring th axe."

"Too heavy."

"I bin totin Dad's rifle!"

A minute more passed. Mark emerged with the stem of a slender tree, freshly cut from the ground and denuded of branches. It was about ten feet long.

Rattler stood up from where he was resting and tried to follow but the rope held firm despite all his jerking and whining.

Mark went straight to the burrow and ran the pole into the opening. Then he twirled and rocked it in the hole. "Lissin fer movement."

Matt slid down, bent over, cocked his head toward the ground and circled the rock pile.

They continued working their respective pole and head but little else happened.

Suddenly the groundhog shot from the burrow, between Mark's legs.

Mark jumped up and sideways. "Dangit!"

Rattler started leaping and barking madly.

The boys looked back behind them. They saw the groundhog loping down the meadow toward the river.

Matt said, "Git a-hint me."

Mark moved behind Matt, squatted on the ground, poked fingers in his ears and watched.

> "I air truly sorry man's domin'on,
> Has broken nature's soc'al union.
> An' jestifies that ill opin'on,
> What makes thee startle at me,
> Thy poor, earth-born compan'on."

While Mark recited Browning, Matt cocked his rifle, assumed a steady stance, aimed, let out a little breath, and squeezed the trigger. PaBOOM!

The little hog had made it halfway to the river when the ground exploded under it. The eruption chucked the animal about a foot into the air. It hit the ground, rolled and lay still.

Mark took his fingers out of his ears. "Nice shootin!" He stood and retrieved Rattler, holding the big dog by the rope. Matt grabbed the part of the rope that was around the dog's neck and the trio staggered downhill toward their quarry, the boys struggling to restrain their dog.

Matt lost his footing and fell onto his butt.

"No gal air a-wantin ter marry a feller what caint stan on his own two feet." Mark said as he waited for Matt to get up.

"No gal air a-wantin ter marry a galoot what hez holes in is overhauls." Matt regained his former upright position and after he spoke he took a swipe at the back of Mark's head, with unqualified success.

"Hole yore jaw. Ow! Golldurn yer!"

They finally reached the groundhog.

Mark took out his Barlow from his sack and began to cut into the critter's stomach to gut it. It was a struggle because that work on the sapling earlier had turned the knife's edge.

Matt queried. "Wrastlin that thar saplin, tucker yer out?"

Mark pulled out the bloody little pocket knife and pointed it at his brother. "Lay off!" He resumed his work, raked the hog's entrails out onto the ground with his fingers and took the hog down to the river to rinse it, his knife, and hands. He was intent on doing this while keeping his feet dry so did not notice Matt walk down to water's edge and scoop up a hand full of mud.

The ball of mud hit Mark square in his right ear.

"AAAH." He fell sideways and both feet shot out from under him and into the water. At the same time, he released the hog and knife to catch his fall.

They both fell into the water.

Mark was instantly up and after Matt. "Damn yore soul ter hell!"

Matt climbed up the bank with some difficulty he was laughing so hard.

Mark caught up with him and punched him hard in a kidney, causing him to pitch forward.

Matt landed on his hands but was up quickly and facing Mark. He swung his left fist around but Mark ducked and punched.

Mark was just out of range and now off balance.

Matt clasped both his hands together and brought them down between Mark's shoulder blades.

That took Mark the rest of the way to the ground. He rolled a couple of times to be sure he was clear and popped back up.

Matt was ready and landed a right hook onto his left ear.

Mark pivoted from the blow, twirled all the way around, bent and charged. He planted his shoulder solidly into Matt's torso.

Both fell, Matt onto his back and Mark on top of him. "Umphph."

While on top Mark pummeled Matt's chest.

Matt rolled to try to get on top of Mark.

Mark grabbed Matt and continued the roll.

They rolled like this a couple more times until Matt was on top and he spread his feet wide to stop. He slipped his left forearm up and pressed it against Mark's neck. At the same time he punched Mark successively in the side of his face.

Mark was busy with both hands trying to move Matt's arm off his neck so he had to take the pounding. He managed to ease Matt's arm up enough to take a breath. Then with all his might he kicked Matt between his outspread legs. That ended the fight.

Matt rolled off, curled up, cupped his groin with both hands and made odd noises as he regained his breath.

Mark just lay flat on his back with an arm over his eyes.

Eventually Matt recovered enough to roll onto his back also.

They remained that way a while, breathing hard and thinking about all the body parts that throbbed.

Mark spoke first. "That air a parful heap er money."

"Yep."

"Aint ne'er heerd a ennybody wit sa much."

"Mor'n enny folks we knows. Aint nuthin ter the coal compny."

Both were quiet again.

Then Mark said, "I still miss Maw an Paw."

Matt could not see this but tears soaked into the sleeve of Mark's union suit.

Matt filled his lungs to capacity with air. There were a few catches as he did so. "I miss em, too."

A tear crept out of Matt's closed right eye.

Mark said, "I air skeerd."

"Me too."

"Ida know what ter do."

"Me nuther."

"I air thinkin city livin would be no pleasure at all."

"I air thinkin the same."

"I knows how ter hannel a bar; don' know hows ter hannel a crowd o people."

"True word."

"I reckon that settles one kest'on."

"Reckon it duz."

After a while Mark spoke again. "Now I gots one other problem ter werk out."

"What be that little bruther?"

"Yore ugly face bein th'onliest thang I see ez a constancy."

Matt howled, then coughed. He rolled over onto his knees, got up on all fours and crawled that way over to Mark. He stood and held out a hand. "Git up. We gots ter fotch yore little knife an cotch that thar whistlepig afore it reaches the falls."

Mark took Matt's hand and struggled up.

Both went back down to the riverbank, arms over each's shoulders.

Rattler joined them from the spot up the meadow where he had retreated once things got too rough for him.

5

John Henry

John Henry enjoyed conversation. He would engage others on just about any topic. He had done this with all his traveling companions. By the time they reached the mine, he knew the family histories of every zebra in the wagon. They called them zebras because they wore white-and-black-striped prison uniforms. They were going to the mine because mine owners could rent convict labor from the State for a whole lot less money than they could hire free men.

And John smiled and joked all the time. He kept all the others on the train and then the wagon highly entertained for the entire trip from Nashville. Every once in a while even a staid guard had to look away to hide a smile or cough to cover a guffaw.

When they entered the narrow little valley John stopped talking long enough to wonder at the steep slopes on both sides of them. This was new. Things were a whole lot flatter in Tipton County where he was from. When they passed through the coal camp, he stopped talking again to look hard at the residents. Although he recognized the poverty, the expressions of distress were new. When they passed the entrance to the mine, he stopped talking to watch hunched over miners enter and others push out little rail carts full of coal. After that he didn't talk much at all.

After that it was up just before sunrise, eat a breakfast of green cornbread and sour red beans, climb into a wagon, ride to the mine, troop down into the depths and hammer rods into the seam of coal to break out chunks, for others to load into little carts and push out. And then out just after dark for more of the same cornbread and beans, a wipe down with a rag soaked in cold water and sleep. Back and forth like that day after day. The cornbread, beans and exercise did wonders for John's physique. The situation did just the opposite for his psyche. His temperament turned as black as the coal he was pounding.

A few years passed like this.

One Friday afternoon the steam whistle blew two hours early. Soon after that twelve African Americans marched by column of twos up a dirt road on the side of a hill devoid of trees. Their black and white striped prison clothes were stiff with dried sweat and coal dust. They shuffled along with ankle chains on. Ahead of them two horses each carried a white guy wearing a crisp law enforcement uniform and carrying a sidearm and a double barrel shotgun. Just behind them two more horses were similarly burdened.

Another zebra walked between his brethren and the two lead guards; John Henry. He was smiling again. They had given him the whole day off, which he had spent eating fresh food and sleeping as much as he could. They let him have soap and hot water for a bath. It turned out to be three baths before John was satisfied he had cleaned out all the coal dust from his ears, nose, teeth and fingernails.

Well above the mine and coal camp, John took frequent deep breaths of clear air. Each deep breath broadened that old smile of his just a little more.

They reached an area that had been scraped flat. The soil there was a shiny dark grey. They marched across this alongside a vertical escarpment colored varying shades of grey and scarred by tool marks.

John realized this used to be the top of a mountain.

Now he could see waves of purple hills beyond the walls of his narrow little valley. John took his shirt off, found a dry spot on the lower half of the back panel and wiped his eyes with it.

The zebras approached a crowd of whites. These had come straight here from the mine, too. Coal dust covered their sweaty faces and hands. They looked as black as the convicts.

This group was loud and rowdy, laughing, joking and jostling each other. Some waved money. One in the middle took money and scribbled notes with a lead pencil onto a scrap of paper.

They all stood next to a steam-powered drill on wheels set up near the edge of the flat. It idled in readiness. "Putt ... putt ... putt ... putt."

One turned and saw the convicts coming. He pounded a neighbor's shoulder and pointed.

Everyone turned, looked at the prisoners and cheered. They continued to joke and jostle, now pointing at the prisoners, who stopped nearby. Their tone turned hostile.

The guards dismounted and unchained all the blacks.

As they were unchained they broke rank and formed a loose circle around John, who was still shirtless, enjoying the breeze around his large, well defined upper body. They spoke encouraging words to him.

"Ye gonter do it, John!"

"Aint no cracker machine can beat yer, John."

"Shore sumthin'll break long afo John be dun."

"Got sumthin especial fer yer, John."

John sought out the voice. "Oh yeah? Whazzat?"

A skinny prisoner came around the crowd from the direction of the whites carrying a sledgehammer in both hands out in front of him as though it were Excalibur and proffered it to John. The hammer's ash handle was clean and white. Its head was shiny and rust free. Stamped on the side of the head was the number 12. John took it, hefted it, looked it over and smiled.

The skinny prisoner said, "Cap'n give it ter yer. S'brand new."

"Well, now. Aint that mighty white o him."

Everyone in his entourage guffawed and cheered.

John led them all to a spot next to the steam drill. There a steel rod stuck out of the ground. Several more six-foot rods lay next to it.

John turned to his followers. "Who air gonter be my shaker?"

Most all of his group raised hands and said things like, "Me, John, me."

Holding his hammer straight out by the grip end as easily as though it were a tack hammer, John pointed to the skinny prisoner. "Riley, you-uns gots a big mout. Git ovah here an git this steel ready."

Everyone laughed and cheered. Those next to him lightly slapped Riley's back and arms and pushed him towards John. Some chanted, "John. John." Some chanted, "Riley. Riley."

Grinning, Riley got on his knees facing the rod sticking out of the ground, grasped it with both hands and jiggled it a little. He gathered the other rods nearer to him and rehearsed how he would grab one and place it on top of the one in the ground.

While Riley did that John took a few easy practice swings at the rod sticking out of the ground, checking his stance and position relative to the rod.

All the blacks turned toward a "whoop" coming from the direction of the drill.

A man dressed in the clothes of industrial middle management stood by the drill. "All right, everybody. Let's get started!" He turned to another fellow similarly dressed standing at the drill's controls. "Harry, the drill ready?"

Harry made an adjustment, causing the drill to putt a little faster. "Ready!"

The manager looked over at John. "John?"

John and Riley were poised at the ready at their rod. "Ready, Cap'n!"

The Manager raised his right hand in the air. "All right, then! First to bury three rods wins! On my mark! One, two, three." He sliced his hand downward. "Go!"

Harry shoved a lever forward and intermittent bursts of steam activated the piston held by a miner atop the rod stuck in the ground beneath it.

Riley started chanting. He accented the first syllable of the second phrase and John hit his rod on the same beat.

"Oh, my hammer. *Ham*mer rang.

Oh, my hammer. *Ham*mer rang."

Everyone in both crowds roared then chattered encouragement to their respective champions.

Both contestants remained even.

During several backswings John warned, "Riley, … ye better be prayin. … If I miss … this steel … terday, … we be buryin yer … termorry!

Everyone laughed, except Riley.

All he could do was widen his eyes. He had to keep cadence.

"Don'cher hear dat hammer. *Ham*mer rang.

Don'cher hear dat hammer. *Ham*mer rang."

The needle in the pressure gauge of the drill crept higher.

John sweat profusely and breathed heavily. His first rod was about two thirds into the ground. "Stop a minit, Riley! Gots ter dry my han's!"

Riley eased back onto his haunches.

John's shirt flew in from his entourage.

John caught it and wiped down.

One of his group brought a bucket of water and offered John a dipper full.

John gulped it and poured another over his head. He dried his hands and the hammer's handle with his shirt and threw it on the ground behind him.

Riley wiped his own face and hands with his own shirttails and gulped a dipper of water offered by the water carrier.

John heard the drill's piston steadily hitting its rod. "Les go, Riley! Les go!"

The water carrier retreated into the crowd.

Riley threw the dipper behind him, grabbed a rod lying on the ground next to him and made ready to place it on top of the first.

John and machine buried the first rod at the same time.

A great roar went up from both groups.

The shaker for each placed another rod on top of the first.

The drill's pressure gauge crept higher.

The mine manager shouted, "Feel the ground shakin, John? That's my drill! That's progress!"

"Naw, Cap'n! Air my hammer suckin win!"

Everyone, Whites and Blacks, laughed.

Riley watched the top of the rod he held, jiggling it a little after each blow.

"Rangin on der mount'n. *Ham*mer rang.

Rangin on der mount'n. *Ham*mer rang."

Harry monitored his machine by ear, making adjustments to levers and wheels by feel.

John pounded as hard as he could, breathing hard and sweating freely.

Harry checked the temperature gauge and hollered. "More coal! More coal!"

A miner brought up a full scuttle and crouched beside Harry's legs on the platform. He flipped open the fire box door and tossed in some lumps.

Fire lashed out around Harry's legs. His pants began to smoke.

John yelled, "Water! Water!"

The man with the bucket rushed up.

John stopped hammering and took a long draught from the dipper. He poured a dipper full over his head and then another over his chest. He went back to work.

"Rangin in heben. *Ham*mer rang.

Rangin in heben. *Ham*mer rang."

A very loud and long high pitched screech caught everyone's attention.

John grinned.

Riley looked up, loosening his grip on the rod and losing his place in the chant.

Just in time John checked his downswing. "Riley, git back ter it! I aint dun yit!"

Riley snapped back to business.

Within a cloud of steam Harry wrenched levers and twisted knobs.

The drill groaned, rattled and slowed as steam spurted from another connection.

The white onlookers shouted at Harry.

The Black onlookers cheered for John.

Riley felt a fierce intensity from hammer, through rod, into his hands. He chanted louder.

"Rangin like jedgment. *Ham*mer rang.

Rangin like jedgment. *Ham*mer rang."

The steam drill started singing in three part discord.

Harry screamed, "Wrap those fittings!"

The stoker ripped his shirt off and took to the nearest leak.

Harry watched gauges, shifted levers and twisted knobs.

The drill released blasts of steam and piercing hisses from several rent connections.

The stoker jumped off.

All the other people near it backed well away.

Stoic Harry remained on post.

The piston butted one last time a rod that was only a little more than halfway buried. The one holding it dropped it and ran off.

John pounded his rod several more times and buried it.

Then he dropped his hammer, grabbed his gut and dropped onto his hands and knees. "Aughk!"

Riley jumped up. "Thas it! Drill only dun one'n a haffen. John whupped down two!"

The prisoners cheered even more and waved uplifted arms.

The miners and the manager shouted at Harry even more.

Harry looked down at his hands, red as boiled lobster claws.

The prisoners raised John up from his crouch on the ground and hoisted him up onto the shoulders of two.

He listed to the left, grimacing and gripping his upper left arm with his right hand. "Aaugh!"

As his supporters paraded him around on their shoulders rejoicing, John relaxed and flopped back onto their heads, both arms outstretched perpendicular to his limp body.

The group stopped, murmured to each other and lowered John onto the ground. They encircled him.

Riley got down on his knees and checked John's breathing and pulse. He leaned back. "He daid." Riley stood back up in the midst of the prisoners.

They all stood looking down at John for a moment.

One crossed John's arms onto his chest and he and seven others picked him up and onto their shoulders, four on each side. They proceeded toward the road that would take them back to their stockade near the coal camp. The other four fell into their column of twos and followed.

Two guards galloped up on their horses jangling handfuls of shackles high in the air. They reined in hard and stopped, then started walking, following the prisoners side by side.

The other two guards on horses came up and fell in behind them.

A cluster of dejected miners followed.

After them came Harry and the mine manager.

The disabled steam drill remained, cooling and ticking as the sun dropped behind the hills.

Close by John Henry's twelve-pound hammer lay where he had dropped it.

6

Mountain Dew

The morning sun of 1889 illuminated the tops of the trees blanketing the hills and vales of the Cumberland Mountains of East Tennessee. The colors of a few trees were beginning to fade.

Sunlight snuck around the myriad leaves of the forest. Passing through the canopy it left a mottled pattern upon a large, ancient, gnarled tree overhanging a bend in a wagon trail.

A middle-aged man dressed in brown-jeans farm clothes rode up to the tree on a mule. He stopped, looked all around, then dismounted. He approached the tree pulling out some paper money from his pants pocket. He placed the money on the ground in a hollow at the base of the tree, reverently flattened it out and retired to his ride. He took its reins and led it on foot farther down the trail around the bend out of sight of the tree. He stopped and waited, continually looking all around him.

Rustling noises startled him. A pair of chipmunks chased each other across the leaves and deadfall. They entertained him for a few minutes before darting down the road.

A heavier crashing really startled him. As he looked in that direction he made to mount up.

A juvenile white tail deer rolled out onto the trail from underneath the bushes on its high side. It stood up on wobbly legs, its eyelids drooping and its tongue hanging out. It looked at the man and mule.

Both looked at the deer and then at each other.

The deer shook its head, wiggled its ears, flapped its big white tail once, snorted and staggered off down the low side of the trail.

The man and his mule stared a moment more after the departing deer.

The mule shook its head.

Then the man led his steed back to the ancient tree.

At the tree he checked the cavity at the base and smiled. He retrieved a shiny ceramic demijohn from the tree's hollow, quickly mounted and rode away.

. . .

Constable Louvin Reilly's office consisted of a stand-up desk in a front corner of Charlie Waggoner's blacksmith shop. This morning Louvin leaned against his desk with his arms folded as a man in the clothes of industrial middle management paced back and forth and complained in an upper Midwest accent.

"I'm tellin ya, Constable, too many o my miners are absent every day, dontcha-know. Or they come in sick. They pose a real danger to themselves and others. A course, my bosses aint too happy about the poor production. They're threatnin to fire me!"

"I air jes one person. Thar be a lotta area ter cover. Law, I caint begin ter know all the hidin places roun here. I air doin everthink I kin."

"I got men that'll help. They're ready anytime you call. I already sent two men out lookin."

"Ye did? When?"

"Bout two weeks ago."

"Whar all they bin?"

"Sent em over to Rocky Top. Heard a rumor shine was comin down from there."

"What all did they found out?"

"Don't know. They aint back yet."

"Aint suprisin. Looky here. Ye gots ter 'low the law ter hannel this."

"Fine! Do somethin soon, or I'll be goin' ta Tazewell an talkin ta Sheriff Hughes!"

The mine manager left Louvin to ponder what to do.

Louvin took the remains of a loaf of bread he had been eating for breakfast and went outside.

The one he was hoping to talk to was on his usual perch.

"Mornin, Jimmie."

Jimmie Brown was sitting on a barrel beside the double doors of the blacksmith's. He was there frequently in the mornings. It was warm there.

As he greeted the boy, Louvin handed him the bread.

Jimmie grabbed it and took two huge bites. It took him a while to chew, develop enough saliva to moisten the bread, then swallow without choking himself. "Thank ee Mr. Reilly."

"How be yore mam?"

"Oh, she be fine, sir. Jes fine."

"How'd er garden do this yar?"

"Bestes speckled beans ever."

"Jimmie, I gots a kest'on fer ye."

"Yessir?"

"Ye 'pear ter know bout lots er thangs what happens roun here."

"Yessir. Knows jes bout everthink what happens roun here."

"What ye hear bout whiskey stills these days?"

"Everthink."

"Good. Good. Cause I gots ter put a stop to em. 'Pears folkses roun here caint tolerate em enny more."

"Its em new folkses comin in here with the mines an churches an sech. Tryin ter change our ways o doin ter suit em."

"True word. ... So, kin ye show me whar them stills be?"

Jimmie finished off the heel of the bread. He took his time. In between bites he said, "Yessir. ... Reckon I could. ... Druther not. ... Them critters git mighty ornery with them what comes snakin roun they bizness."

"Reckon thas fair. How bout this. Can ye jes tell me whar they be?"

"Reckon so."

A minute passed. Louvin asked, "Well?"

"Heerd bout one west a here. Mebbe bout a mile or so off. Up off the road ter the Gap. In a narrow holler wit a sprang comin out the ground. Heap o birch trees in thar."

Louvin thought about those directions, then realized something. "Air that 'bove my place?"

Jimmie swallowed the last bite of bread. ... "Yessir."

Louvin adjusted his hat and rubbed the back of his neck. "Thank ee, Jimmie, Thank ee. Now, would ee do sumthin else fer me?"

"Yessir?"

"Go an tell Homer Magill and Silas Kent ter come here ter Charlie's soon's they kin. Tell em each ter brang a axe an a shotgun."

"Yessir. I will." Jimmie stood up on the barrel and from there mounted his old sway back mule that was dozing against the wall of the shop beside him. He jiggled the reins and the mule moved away from the wall. He tugged on the reins to turn the mule's head toward the cross road running alongside Eli Parch's Mercantile. He shook the reins and stirred the animal into a slow walk.

Louvin figured it would be close to dark before Homer and Silas showed up.

It was just midday. That still afforded them plenty of time. "Thank ee fer comin. Jimmie tell yer what I aim ter do?"

Homer exclaimed, "Gonter raid us a still!"

"Right."

Silas asked, "Who's?"

Both Louvin and Homer looked at him.

Silas looked back at them and then down at the ears on his horse. "Reckon that aint important."

Louvin mounted up. "Les haid fer the Gap."

After Eli's and Charlie's places were out of sight Homer asked, "Whar it be?"

Louvin told him what Jimmie had said.

Homer pondered that and then said, "That up above yore place?"

"Blieve so."

70

"This whole place has dun got set plum catawampus. Folkses drivin their critters ter death. Chillen killin chillen. Moonshine flowin like water. Luvin, 'pears ter me ye dun loss all yore grip. Mebbe it air bout time fer a new con-stable roun here. A man a might more intersted, an younger, an sech."

Louvin adjusted his hat. He almost rubbed the back of his neck. He was aware it was hot. He knew the answer to this question. "Have ye ennybody in mind, Homer?"

"A course, Me."

"Tell yer what. Nex chance ye git, ride on down ter Tazewell, yander ter the Sheriff's office an 'ply fer the job."

"That all thar is ter it?"

"Well, Sheriff Hughes'll want ter talk wit yer. An he air perty perticlar. Bein a elected official, he may be lookin et someone else. But, that thar be how ye start."

Homer thought a moment. "Aint meanin no disrespect, Luvin."

"No offense takin, Homer. … Les leave our hosses here an go the rest er the way on foot."

They dismounted in front of Louvin's cabin and laid their reins over sundry implements in front.

Louvin's daughter Lucy Lee came out of the cabin. "Hey, Paw. Hey, Homer, Silas." She saw how they were outfitted. "You-uns headed fer the still?"

Homer said, "Jimmie Brown 'lows as thar be one up 'bove yore cabin."

"Thought I smelt one when the afternoon breeze drapt off the hill back a hyar."

Homer said, "As I said."

Lucy asked, "What?"

Louvin said, "Ne'er mind. This a way." He struck off around the side of his cabin, across a pasture in the back. Halfway across he realized someone was missing. He looked back.

Homer was still talking to Lucy. He was talking; she was shaking her head. Finally, he shrugged, tipped his hat and trotted up to Louvin and Silas.

Louvin could not restrain the little smirk. "Les haid inter these here woods. Keep quiet. Don' say nary a word." There were three reasons Louvin didn't want Homer talking.

He continued leading them uphill into deeper woods. It was steep and brushy; talking would have been difficult anyway.

They continued in silence for a half mile. They stopped halfway up in a dell and took a moment to allow hearts and lungs to normalize.

Louvin got close to his posse and whispered. "The still air in the next holler over. We kin snake up this side. Spread out. An be quiet!"

Homer and Silas did as he bade.

Once they were about twenty feet apart from each other they all ascended the side of the dell. They all reached the ridge line at about the same time. All got on hands and knees, then on tummies and crawled to the crest. Each picked out a bush or log to crawl up behind.

Once settled, Louvin took his hat off and eased around his bush to peer over into the hollow. He saw nothing but a mossy barrel by a birch tree on the other side of the brook created by the spring. He scanned up and down the hollow three times to make sure his brain was properly coordinating with his eyes.

"Luvin, they aint no still hyar!" As loud as he could Homer confirmed what Louvin saw. "No still hyar!" echoed back to make sure Louvin got the message.

"I sees."

"I leff everthink whar it fell ter come out here fer nuthin!?"

"'Pears so."

"If that don' jes beat all I ...."

"Looks like sumthin's bin down thar." Silas finally spoke up.

"Les go down an look roun." Louvin talked a little louder than usual. "We kin start up thar at the top er the holler an werk our way down. Ennybody sees anythin, jes call out an lemme take a look fust afor ye touch it!"

They regrouped, moved to the spring, spread out again and started walking downhill and looking around at the ground. They saw footprints, hoof prints, wagon wheel ruts and a spot where a fire had been.

Louvin went over to the mossy barrel, took off the piece of canvas covering its top and reeled back. Methane the odor of rancid wash boiled forth and nearly knocked him out.

"Bin gone two, (cough), mebbe tree, weeks."

"Luvin, whatjer make er this?"

Luvin turned to see Silas holding up a woman's bonnet.

The morning sun crept above the mountain tops and began warming the roofs of Eli Parch's Mercantile and Charlie Waggoner's smithy. The only life in the roads were two mules that stood hitched to a teamster's wagon in the shadow beside Eli's store. It was loaded with sacks of sugar and barrels of molasses.

Behind the rig one of the doors to Eli's storeroom was open. Just inside two men were barely visible. One was dressed in store clerk clothes. As he watched out the door he held his hand out.

The other wore brown jeans and laid paper money into the first's open hand. The farmer type finally stopped shelling out money.

Eli looked at the stack, nodded to the farmer and with some difficulty stuffed the money into his pants pockets, again looking out into the road.

The farmer looked out too but just grinned. He held a finger into the air, remembering something and walked out. He walked to the front of the wagon. He reached under the seat and withdrew a bulky burlap bag. He carried that back into the storeroom. He returned to Eli, partially withdrew a gallon sized demijohn, replaced it and handed the whole kit over. He smiled, tipped his hat and exited the storeroom.

Eli held the bag and brown jug behind him and followed his customer to the door. He peered side to side, up and down the road.

The farmer returned to and climbed in the front of the wagon, sat, took up the reins and urged the mules out into the middle of the road, turning right. He drove between the buildings, down the slope toward the mill, across the ford in the stream just below the mill and turned left down the road alongside the far bank of the stream, disappearing into the woods.

Louvin had been out all day trying to find Cotton Joe to serve him with papers. Cotton Joe had tightly curled white hair, pale skin and pink eyes. He was a local resident whom everyone referred to as "tetched."

According to the mother of the bride, he crashed her daughter's wedding reception wild and drunk. As he proclaimed his love for her daughter, he ran through the crowd and overturned tables, including the one with the wedding cake. He got away before anyone could catch and hold him down. Momma had filed a complaint with Squire Bateman.

Louvin had had no success finding Joe, so was returning to the settlement. As he rode he fretted over the big fight he had had recently with his nephews Matthew and Mark Johnson over their lack of direction. Ever since their parents had died, Louvin had tried to serve as parent to them. That was difficult; they were so independently minded. Both boys were nearly past age and not married yet. They had inherited a mountain that the local coal company badly wanted. To Louvin's way of thinking, with that amount of money, the boys could conquer the world. Nevertheless, they seemed perfectly content to do nothing but hunt, fish and trap.

Louvin approached Eli's and Charlie's late that day and saw a group of miners in the road. They were still smudged and sweaty from work.

One of them was hovering over Eli, who was sitting on his porch, back against the wall, knees up under his chin, and arms wrapped around his shins. "Tell us whar tis! I know yer know! Ye bin sellin surplies to im!"

Louvin spurred his horse right up, dismounted and strode right into the middle of the group of riled miners. "What kinder doins air this!? Eli, you-uns hart!?"

One of the miners behind him rabbit punched him in the back below his neck.

He staggered forward into another miner, who delivered an upper cut that knocked him flat on his back. That jarred his revolver out of its holster. He rolled onto his stomach and pushed himself up as quickly as he could. He felt for his weapon. Discovering an empty holster, he just lunged at the nearest miner.

They collided; but another miner pulled Louvin away and swung him around into yet another miner. This began a session of pushing Louvin from one to another. They laughed, socked and kicked him.

He became disoriented, flailing his arms trying to land a solid punch.

A loud pa-BOOM rang out close by, and everyone dropped flat onto the ground.

As he dropped, the one who had been harassing Eli grabbed the left side of his head and screamed. Blood flowed out from between his fingers.

Mark Johnson ran up and picked up Louvin's revolver. He cocked and aimed it at the miners and helped Louvin up. "Ye hart, Uncle?"

Louvin straightened up and rolled his shoulder blades. "I'm okay."

Matt Johnson came up, installing a fresh percussion cap in his 1861 Springfield. He aimed it at the miners. "Ye fairin okay, Uncle Luvin? Mr. Parch?"

"Yeah. I air fine. Though twas a right tussle. Thank ee boys."

"That varmint whats missin is ear slapped me! Hard!" Eli whined.

Louvin took control. "I'll ax ye agin. What sort o cussed mischief air all o this!?"

The miners remained quietly flat on the ground, looking up at the array of armament pointed at them.

The wounded leader finally said, "We wanted a little shine thas all. I know this here varmint sells a heap o sugar an molasses, so ter my way o thinkin he knows whar a still be."

"Why air you-uns lookin sa hard at gittin yore load on?"

"We all loss a bodac'ous bet terday at the mine. Was set on gittin shut o the week arly." The wounded leader took his hand away from the side of his head and looked at it. "I gots ter have sum hep here."

Although his ear now sported a shallow notch at the top, it was bleeding a lot, as ears are wont to do.

Louvin ordered, "Eli, git sum band-ages outer yore store."

Eli just sneered at the wounded miner.

"I'll pay fer em!"

Eli hopped up and stomped inside. A moment later he emerged with a roll and tossed it onto the porch in front of the casualty.

Another miner came up and attended to his leader's head.

"Now, all o yer set out fer yore homes!" Louvin ordered.

Everyone rose to go. The leader wasn't quite ready to turn it loose. "Con-stable, ye gots ter a-rrest that cussed varmint what tried ter kill me!"

Louvin replied, "If he'd a-wanted ter peg yer, he'd a dun it."

Matt added, "I hit what I aimt fer."

Another miner who heretofore had been silent spoke. "That was sum parful close shootin, son. What air yore name?"

"Johnson. Matthew Johnson."

Yet another miner got interested. "I heerd o sum bruthers o that name in the war. Gots ter be right re-nowned fer their shootin."

Just about everyone nodded.

"Thems were my paw an his bruther."

This time everyone did nod.

Louvin was ready to go home and go to bed. "If yer want ter press charges, come back here termorry wit yore boss man Mr. Moore. An be shore ter tell im bout ternight!"

That persuaded all the miners to depart.

Louvin turned on Eli. "Ye want ter press charges?"

"Naw. Reckon not!"

"Awright, whar it be?

"What!?"

"That thar still!"

"Caint say as I knows, zactly!"

"Do yore bestes, or I'll shet ye down, too!"

"Alls I knows is ye take that thar road aside the stream b'low the mill. Thars an ol' holler tree at a bend in the road. Put money in th' holler an go roun the bend. After a minit come back an fotch yore likker from outer the holler."

"Dint know zactly, eh? Fine. Matt, Mark, ye minded ter hep me termorry?"

Mark seemed extra interested. "Shore, Uncle!"

"Thanks agin fer heppin me out ternight."

"Twernt nuthin."

Matt added, "We caint stay riled at yer, Uncle. We luvs yer an knows ye luv us. Everthink happnin roun here of late has tried us sumthin fierce."

"I gots ter git home fer supper. Meet yer at Charlie's at daybreak. G'night."

Mark decocked Louvin's pistol and returned it to him. "G'night, Uncle Luvin."

Matt put his rifle on half cock. "Mr. Parch, ye want us ter stay whilst ye close up?"

"Naw, thank ee!" Eli thought a moment and elected to soften his attitude. "Er. Naw boys. Thank ee. I air fine, now."

Louvin mounted his horse and rode away. The Johnson boys mounted their mule and rode off in the opposite direction. Eli watched Louvin until he disappeared into the trees, kicked a post supporting the roof of his porch then stomped into his store.

Morning sunlight snuck around the myriad leaves of the forest, casting tiny shadows upon the old silent sentinel at the bend in the trail.

A man in oversized farm clothes rode up on a mule. A grey slouch hat obscured the top of his face. A large bandana around his neck covered the bottom. He dismounted and straightaway went to the tree, laid some money into the hollow and led his animal around the bend.

Moments later a ripple of shaking leaves began a ways up the hill above the tree and moved to the bottom of the thicket. A short person emerged from the rhododendron, carrying a pair of demijohns. This one was also hiding inside an oversized coat, slouch hat and bandanna. He went to the tree, retrieved the money, left one demijohn and headed back up the hill.

Louvin's voice nearby caused the vendor to pause. "Stop rat thar in the name er th' law!"

The vendor disappeared up the fairly well-beaten path into the rhododendron thicket.

Louvin came up and also disappeared into the thicket.

Branches shook and jerked.

The sound of human grunts and cracking branches emerged through the leaves.

Louvin and the vendor rolled together back down the hill onto the road, followed by a loose demijohn.

The vendor cried out in a female voice. "Ow! Git off, yer galoot!"

Louvin jumped off and stood.

The woman sat up and grabbed her elbow. As she did her hat fell off.

Louvin took another step back. "Katy!?"

"Ye migh nigh a-broke my arm!"

"Sorry, dint know ye was a gal."

"Oh, thank ee kinely!"

Matt and Mark ran up. Matt was wearing the baggy clothes, slouch hat and bandanna. They stopped short.

Mark asked, "Katy!?"

Matt elbowed Mark in the arm and sniggered.

"Uh, hello, Mark. Would ye hep me up?"

"Uh, uh, shore." Mark rushed over and helped Katy to her feet.

Louvin spoke. "So, it air yore pap what's runnin the still."

Katy said nothing. She just rubbed her sore elbow and looked at Mark.

Louvin continued. "Awright. Les go. Take us ter im."

"Yessir." She started back up the trail into the rhododendron.

Mark followed, then Louvin.

Matt picked up the loose jug and brought up the rear, chuckling.

The same man that had bought sugar and molasses from Eli Parch filled two leaky wooden buckets with water from a mountain stream. Ropes were tied to their bails. The other ends of the ropes were tied to the ends of a pole. As he stood he placed the pole across his shoulders and lifted the entire assembly. He turned and walked to a wooden barrel nearby and emptied both buckets into it, which brought the barrel full.

A coil of copper tubing stuck out of the water.

The man set the buckets down and took a dipper hanging from a nail in the side of the barrel. He stooped down next to a woman, looking about the same age as he, who was filling a demijohn with the clear liquid flowing from a copper tube sticking out of the side of the barrel near the bottom.

They nodded at each other and he winked at her.

As she pulled her full demijohn away he caught the flow in his dipper. As he pulled that away from the flow the woman slipped an empty demijohn in place. No spillage.

He took a sip and grimaced. "Perfect."

He stood, hung the dipper up, and picked up two corked demijohns sitting next to the woman. He carried those to a canvas tarpaulin covering a mound. He lifted a corner of the tarpaulin to reveal more jugs. He placed the latest with those. As he was holding up the tarp Katy's voice from above took his attention away from his inventory.

"Paw, we gots truble!"

Katy's father dropped the corner of the tarp, looked all around and found Katy, Mark, Louvin and Matt standing on the ridge above looking down at him.

The woman filling demijohns likewise looked up and then back down at another girl looking a little older than Katy.

This one had been tending a fire under a metal cylindrical container with a conical top and copper tubing affixed to the apex. She was now looking up at the group on the ridge with her right hand gripping a Colt Army .44 holstered at her side over her cotton print dress.

Katy's father took another look all around. He appeared relieved there was no more to Louvin's posse than the Johnson boys.

Louvin proclaimed, "It air the law, Donal Daly. Come ter shet yer down."

Donal walked over to a pile of chopped and split wood next to a wooden barrel with a folded tarpaulin covering its top. He picked up a couple of pieces. "Man gots a right ter 'arn a livin, Luvin."

"Man kin earn a honest livin that don' hurt other folks."

Donal carried the wood over to the older girl and dropped them by her feet.

She picked one up with her left hand and poked spots in the fire under the boiler. She did this only half looking at the fire. She kept most of her attention on the group on the ridge. She kept her right hand on her revolver.

Donal continued. "Folks want what I gots. I provides it ter em."

Louvin returned. "Aint talkin bout them; talkin bout thar famlies an sech."

Donal walked back to the wooden barrel next to the wood pile. "Livin air hard roun here. If a feller aint bustin rocks ter draw corn off sum mountin, he air bustin rocks ter draw coal outer its innards." As he talked he removed the tarp off the top of the barrel. He bent over the barrel close to the open top and took a deep whiff. He

80

closed his eyes, turned his head slightly, smiled and nodded. "What I gots eases thar aches an misry."

"All true. An right poetic ter boot. But times air a-changin roun here. Folkses air gittin more civlized. They aint a-wantin this here nefar'ous backwoods bizness."

"Sa free country, Luvin. Ye oughter 'low free enterprise ter decide."

"Donal, I air a-comin back here termorry mornin with more men, guns an axes. If ye air still here, we will ax yore still an a-rrest yer an yer whole famly. Louvin glanced at Katy.

Katy tightened her grip on Mark's hand.

"Awright, awright! Katy come on down an hep yore suster Corey."

The older girl dropped the smoking stick she had been poking the fire with, took one of the buckets by the water barrel, filled it therefrom and poured the contents onto the fire under the boiler.

Excited steam and ash billowed about her.

Maggie Daly continued to hold a demijohn under the spout, as she had done throughout Louvin and Donal's exchange. As the flow stopped, she corked the jug and carried it to the pile under the tarp.

Katy started down the hill and Mark started to follow.

Louvin asked, "Mark, whar air ye a-goin?"

Katy and Mark stopped and looked back. "Wit Katy."

Louvin and Matt looked at each other and back at Mark. "Aint ye heerd what I was jes a-sayin?"

"Don' keer. Alls I knows rat now is I wants ter be wit Katy."

Katy smiled at Mark and hugged his arm.

Louvin looked at them a moment. Enlightenment relaxed his face. "Oh! Uh. Huh. Awright, I reckon. Eh. See yer back ter the settlement?"

"Spose." Mark and Katy turned to go down to the still.

Louvin and Matt turned to head back to the road.

Louvin stopped and turned around. "Wait!"

Katy and Mark stopped and looked back.

Donal and Maggie looked up.

Louvin unbuttoned the front of his shirt and slipped in a hand.

Corey drew her revolver half out of its holster.

Louvin withdrew the bonnet Silas had found at the old still site and tossed it to Katy. "'Pears ter me like this might belong ter yore suster."

7

The Mail Train

If one had been awake that late and out there, one would have felt the little earthquake. A little quake would not be surprising. These were mountains. One could always expect a little slip along a seam or little sag within a cavern.

The quake was just strong enough to loosen a bit of the edge of a flat near the summit of a small mountain. Rocks and dirt slid down the side, gaining momentum, more rocks and more dirt. In a short time all was quiet and still again. Another flat at the bottom of the hill caught all the debris. Unfortunately, that flat was not meant for that. It was meant more for the railroad tracks.

Constable Louvin Reilly was out serving papers for Justice of the Peace Harold Bateman. His nephew on his wife's side Matthew Johnson was along for the company. Their animals plodded along. The men said nothing. They had ended their discourse on work, the weather and local gossip a while ago. Louvin really wanted to talk to Matthew about his plans for the future, but knew that would rile him, and he for sure did not want to spoil the good mood they both were in.

Matt wanted to talk to Louvin about his future, too. But he was afraid Louvin would get pushy and rile him. Louvin was the only adult Matt felt close to. About twelve years ago both Matt's parents died when their cabin caught fire in the middle of the night. He and his younger brother Mark had been fending for themselves ever since. But even though he and Mark were doing well on their own, Matt had recently begun to long for some mentoring by someone older.

In the distance a train whistle blew.

Louvin said, "Mail train." He looked skyward toward the sun. "Tad late."

The train whistle continued to blow.

Louvin and Matt frowned at each other.

The whistle transformed into horrendous noises of crashing metal and wood, an explosion, then rushing steam.

Louvin and Matt reined in and listened. They of course looked in the direction of the noises, but saw nothing but a mile of trees.

Once things were quiet Louvin told Matt, "High back ter the settlemint an git Mark! An everone else ye kin find! I'll put out straight fer the train! Giddap!" He heeled his horse and galloped off.

Matt turned his filly and heeled her hard. She jumped into a gallop toward the consortium of mill, blacksmith, and general store.

Louvin raced along the mountain road as fast as the hills, curves and ruts would allow. He reached a flatter section of the road running through some woods. He emerged from the woods and reined in hard, nearly twisting his horse's neck back double. The horse protested but stopped.

Spread before him in the clearing two broken up freight cars lay in a heap on and around the tracks. Half buried underneath them was a coal tender lying on its side across the tracks. Jackknifed against it was a steam locomotive lying on its side.

Smoke billowed from the broken stack and drive platform. Flames darted within the smoke around the roof and through the windows of the platform. Steam hissed through several ruptures along the body of the engine. Debris and coal lay all over the ground.

Louvin heeled his horse forward. "Giddap!" He galloped up to the wrecked cars and reined in hard again. "Halloo! Ennybody thar!?" Hearing nothing he heeled his horse on toward the engine. He stopped, peered through the smoke around the drive platform and called again. "Halloo! Eng'neer! Yer thar?"

From the other side of the wreckage came a faint human voice. It was someone moaning. No, it was someone singing.

Louvin looked around to pinpoint it, dismounted and ran to the drive platform and looked in, dodging the flames issuing from the fire box. He finally located the source on through the platform.

Lying on his back against the hillside on the other side of the engine from Louvin was a man wearing heavy denim coveralls. They were charred and smoking. The remnants of the gloves he had been wearing still hosted some flames.

A gash along his hairline oozed tarry blood. His face and hands were burned and bloody. His eyes stared into the sky.

Louvin clambered as quickly as he could through the gap between the engine and tender. He couldn't avoid taking in a couple breaths of smoke. He fell to his knees by the engineer, coughing and wiping his eyes on his shirt sleeve. "Don' try an move. Ye'll be awright here. Far seems ter be dyin down. More folks air a-comin soon." Louvin looked back and forth along the wreck. "Whars yore farman?"

"Saw them thar rocks. ... Tole im ter jump. ... He shook is haid. ... Pushed im off." The engineer tried to chuckle but coughed a spray of blood instead.

Louvin pulled out a handkerchief and wiped the engineer's face. "Ennyone else on board? I bes check on em.""

"Naw. Jes me."

"What be yore name, son?"

"Alley. George Alley."

"Luvin."

"Pleased ter meet yer, Luvin. Wisht I looked better fer yer ... felt better."

"Don' fret none bout that. Jes git easy an holt on; ye gonter be fine."

"Luvin?"

"Yeah?"

"Tell my mam I luv er."

"Ye kin tell er yersef directly."

George relaxed into the rocky bank as though it were his own feather bed at home. He started singing again.

"Though like the wanderer, the sun gone down,

85

Darkness be over me, my rest a stone;
Yet in my dreams I'd be, nearer, my God, to thee;
Nearer, my God, to thee, nearer to thee."

George relaxed even more, exhaled one final time and stared up toward Heaven.

Louvin stood. He looked again end to end at the wreckage, ending at the front end of the engine. He picked up the dead engineer and struggled with him through rocks, and uplifted ties and around that end of the wreck. Getting around to the other side he took the body a good ways beyond the debris field and laid it down beneath a tree. He took his hat off and rubbed the back of his neck. He bent over and closed George's eyes.

He turned back to the wreckage, trotted over to the freight cars and began dragging pieces of siding away from the tracks. He became progressively frantic in this process. A man's voice startled him.

"Laws a mercy! Laws a mercy! Gawge? Whars Gawge?"

Louvin looked up the tracks and spied a large African American limping toward him, wincing every once in a while. "Ye the farman?"

He nodded. "Ye seen Gawge?"

"Yeah." Louvin pointed. "Over yander. Sorry."

"Oh, great gosh in heben!" The fireman passed Louvin without pausing and made his way to his engineer, sniffling and blubbering.

While the fireman knelt and made over his engineer's body, Louvin grappled a half crushed crate jammed under a freight car, muttering under his breath. After tugging on it a moment he stopped to heed Matt's voice.

"Uncle!" Matt rode up.

"Matt, whars Mark? Git back ter the settlemint an tell everone thar ter git down here, now! We gots ter clear these here tracks!"

"Awready dun. Should be here enny time, now." As he spoke Matt dismounted and began tugging on the crate Louvin was having trouble with.

Together they managed to extract it and slide it away from the tracks. They next chose a side door that had been knocked off the freight car. It was too heavy for them.

Suddenly Cindy Grove appeared. "What kin I do?"

Matt smiled. "Hey, Cindy."

Cindy greeted. "Hey Matt; hey Mr. Reilly."

Louvin forgot for a moment what was all about him and smiled. "Hello, Cindy. Ennyone else a-comin?"

"Yessir. A passel."

The three of them set to the door and managed to drag it away.

Louvin took a break but Cindy and Matt started on sacks of mail. As they picked up sacks together they smiled at each other.

Louvin heard hoof beats, squeaking wheels and human voices behind him. He turned to greet Mark Johnson and Katy Daly, leading virtually everyone else that lived in the area. They rode horses, mules and wagons.

They straightaway converged on the wreckage. They parked their wagons close to the freight cars. Some climbed inside and tossed bags and mail car accessories out into the wagons. Some picked up lumps of coal off the ground and tossed them into the wagons.

Pastor Brown, his wife Eleanor and Nellie Oxford went straight to the engineer and fireman.

Louvin looked up at the sun and shook his head. "We air runnin outer time!" He shouted to the crowd, "We air runnin outer time; werk faster!"

Squire Bateman and two others struggled with a pair of freight car wheels. He yelled at Louvin. "Luvin, everone air doin the bestes they kin! Leastways, we aint got nuthin here twill move that thar tender an engine!"

"Shore we do! All these people, beastes an rope! It air gots ter be enuff!"

"Sorry, Luvin. Afeared not."

Mark stopped his work and looked around. "I air thinkin the same, Uncle."

"We jes gots ter try. No one knows fer shore. Jes gots ter try. Everbody! Lissin here! We air gonter move that thar engine! Take all the rope. Git all them critters over thar an hitch em up!"

Everyone turned their attention to Louvin. Then they looked at the engine. They did nothing.

"Git ter it! Time air a-wastin!"

Those handling rope and animals unhitched everything and began attaching it to the engine. They hesitated at times, comparing the massive weight to their puny resources.

Louvin strode over. "Awright! Tighten up them lines! Thas it! On three! One ... two ... three!

Everyone and everything heaved.

The engine did not move.

They all relaxed.

"Do it agin! One ... two ... three!"

Everyone and thing tightened and strained again, trying harder and longer this time.

A rope snapped and everyone on that line ducked, covered their heads with hands and scurried away from the flying end.

The engine did not budge.

"Pitiful! Pitiful! Put yore backs inter it!"

No one moved. They all just looked at Louvin and back at the engine. Many looked down at the ground.

A commotion nearby caused them all to look from the engine up the tracks. What they saw made them all shout for joy.

About twenty miners walked down the tracks toward the train wreck. Leading them was the local mine manager himself. In the back were twelve of the convict labor force dressed in their black and white striped clothes. Trailing them were four guards on horseback. All surrounded sixteen mules hitched together in teams of eight. The trailing team pulled a long flatbed cart loaded with railroad rails and ties, spikes, coils of cable and assorted tools.

They reached the wreck and forthwith set to work with the manager directing the operation. One group led one team of mules to the engine. One group unhitched the trailing team from the cart and led it to the engine. Others grabbed cable and headed to the engine where they lay segments over the boiler and fastened the ends to sturdy components of the undercarriage near the ground. The men with the mules fastened the other ends of the cables to the teams. They similarly hitched up some of the healthier looking farm animals.

Then, upon the manager's commands, they all heaved.

The engine rolled over onto its top.

Everyone cheered.

With one more little tug the animals rolled the engine the rest of the way over onto its other side. It was now safely away from the road bed, laying within a huge cloud of dust and the echo off the hillside of the spectacular sound it made when it hit the ground.

Everyone's cheers surmounted the echo.

Louvin yelled to Bateman. "What air the time?"

Bateman pulled his watch out and looked at it. "Twenty ter three."

"Oh, Lordy, time air mighty short!" Louvin looked around and focused on Matt, who with Cindy was attaching ropes to the tender. "Matt, come here!"

Matt and Cindy looked around.

Louvin gestured to come.

Matt ran over to him. "Yessir?"

"Matt, ye gots ter take a hoss up them thar tracks an warn the passenger train."

"Yessir, Uncle."

They looked around the scene. Every animal and human was engaged in the cleanup.

"Any idee which one. 'Pears like they all be occypied."

His own horse was presently tied to the coal tender.

Something caught Louvin's attention that made him laugh out loud.

Jack Davy rode up on his thoroughbred stallion. Davy was an Englishman who had recently arrived in the area to negotiate purchases of land from the residents for the coal company he represented. He was especially interested in the Johnson boys' mountain. He was also very proud of his horse. He was quite successful racing it.

"Constable, is there anything I can assist you with?"

"Thar shore is; give Matt yore hoss ter ride up these tracks ter warn the passenger train."

"I am sorry, Constable. I cannot do that. He would break a leg on those tracks. He is too valuable."

"Hoss aint worth all the folkses in danger here an on that thar passenger train. It'll be roarin through here enny minit!"

"Absolutely not! I see plenty of horses here. Take one of them."

"Then you-uns ride up thar an stop the train!"

"As I said! Loose ballast! Uneven ties! Even I could not keep him safe!"

With his left hand Louvin grabbed both reins close to the horse's mouth. With his right hand he drew his Navy .36, cocked it and pointed it at Davy's left eye. "I air takin this hoss in the name er the law! Git off! Now!"

Davy stiffened and eased back in his saddle. He released the reins, raised both his hands in the air and stared at the bore of the revolver. He disengaged his feet from the stirrups, swung his right leg over the horse and slid off onto the ground, all the while with hands in the air and eyes on the revolver.

Louvin ordered, "Step away from that beast. Matt, hop on up thar an ske-daddle."

Davy backed away a few feet.

Louvin maintained aim at Davy's eye.

Matt climbed aboard the horse. "Don' fret none, Mr. Davy. I knows a short cut. Yeeeehaaaah!" Matt ground his brogans hard into the thoroughbred's sides and pulled a set of reins to turn it.

The horse protested at the brutish handling but jumped into an immediate gallop.

They rode, not along the tracks, but up the road alongside it and disappeared into the trees.

Davy said, "If any harm comes to that animal, Sheriff Hughes will be the first to know!"

Louvin decocked and holstered his revolver. "Figger that'll better yore bargnin posit'on! Now, ye either len a han over thar wit my friens or git the hell outer my sight."

"Well, I am certainly not leaving. Not until that lump gets back with my horse."

"Suit yersef!" Louvin turned and was delighted to see that while he had been engaged with Matt and Davy, the rest of the crowd had dragged the tender away from the tracks.

Now fourteen men were carrying a rail over to where ones had been torn loose. Others followed with picks, shovels, spike pullers, cant hooks and mauls.

He joined a group who were removing rocks off the tracks.

Davy sought out a tree and sat down in its shade.

Louvin was puzzling over a six foot steel rod he had pulled from the rubble when a long blow from a train whistle stopped him and everyone else dead still.

They all looked toward the sound, not moving, barely breathing.

A locomotive pulling a tender and two passenger cars slowly chugged down the tracks. As it got closer to the wreck site it slowed more and more, finally stopping with a whoosh just feet away from the flat car.

Numbers of passengers sprouted halfway out of the windows of the cars looking at the spectacle. They pointed and chattered with each other.

Jack Davy stood up and craned his neck looking all around the train and its vicinity.

Louvin tossed the rod aside and, always looking at the new arrivals, walked toward them.

As he reached the drive platform, the engineer had his head out. "Did George make it?"

"Huh? Oh. Naw. Sorry." Louvin didn't even look at him. He just kept studying the faces of the passengers sticking out of windows or standing on the ground.

The engineer hung his head and shook it, then looked back up. "How bout Jack?"

That got Louvin's attention. "Jack? Oh, the farman. Yeah, 'pears ter be okay. Mighty de-sturbed bout George."

"What happint?"

Louvin returned to looking at the crowd of passengers standing by the train. "Rock slide." Then he smiled and walked on beyond the engineer.

A brawny young man wearing a watch cap and long wool coat and carrying a duffle bag over his shoulder stepped down out of a doorway of the last passenger car. He faced toward the wreck site. He flashed a great smile, dropped his bag and trotted forward. He met Louvin and hugged him.

Louvin hugged back and held the fellow tight for a moment.

They finally broke off and Louvin stood back with his hands still on the young man's shoulders. "Welcome home, John. Come on. Lucy Lee bin mos' crazed a-waitin fer ye."

. . .

An apple hung from its twig on a branch on its tree growing next to a single pen log cabin far from any railroad tracks.

Matthew Johnson's hand reached up and plucked it off. It carried the fruit down to Jack Davy's horse's mouth.

The horse scarfed it whole from Matt's outstretched hand.

The voice of a young boy behind him caught Matt's attention and he turned to see little Jimmie Brown on his mule.

"Mat-tew Johnson!"

"Jimmie Brown! ... Who air wit yer?"

Sitting behind Jimmie was Jack Davy.

Jimmie said, "This here Ainglish feller air a-lookin fer is hoss."

Jack was already off the mule. He trotted up to his horse slapping dust off the seat of his jodhpurs. He straightaway began examining all the horse's legs and feet.

"Reckon ez e fund im." Jimmie observed.

While Jack continued to examine his horse all over, Jimmie and Matt conversed.

Jimmie started, "Johnny Oxford an Jimmy Randall were tried yander ter Tazewell fer the killin o their gals."

"That so?"

"Yessir. Johnny got twenty yar; but Jimmy was a-set loose."

"Fer sartain?"

"Strue. An the mail train wrecked down b'low the mine yestiddy. Rock slide."

"War it bad?"

"Kilt th' eng'neer. Farman air safe, though. Passenger train bout runned inter it, but it stopped jes in time."

"That air good."

"E'en better, Lucy Lee's John was onter that thar passenger train. He dun come home fer good from a-werkin them thar boats on the Cummerlin River."

"That air fustrate news."

"Strue. He an Miss Lucy plan ter git hitched in a month's time."

"That soon?"

Of course, Matt knew all of this already, but let Jimmie go on. Jimmie loved his work as the community's self-appointed town crier. Too bad he was too poor to own a bell.

"Matt, ye mine iffen I git a couple o them thar apples offen yore tree?"

"Naw. Course not. Git all yer a-minded ter."

Jimmie slid off his mule, creating a little cloud of dust off the back and sides of the animal, and trotted up to the apple tree that was growing next to Matt and Mark's cabin. He began gathering all he could hold in the front of his shirt.

Matt walked over to a hand-hewn bench beside the front door of his cabin to retrieve Jack's tack.

A barefoot Cindy Grove sat there, too. As Matt approached, she wiped juice off her chin with the back of her hand holding a half-eaten apple, proffered the apple to Matt, and batted her eyes.

Matt grinned.

As he bent down to pick up the tack, she kissed his cheek.

As he walked back to Jack's horse he wiped his cheeks with his shoulders hoping that would cure his blushing. He was fine with his uncontrollable grin.

As Jack continued to examine his horse, he spoke. "Don't see anything. No cuts. No swelling even." He straightened up, patted his horse on its side and examined its mane. "You brushed him out?"

"Yessir. Cleaned im up an fed im after all er yestiddy's commotion."

"He's in fine condition. It appears you know something about such an animal after all."

"Aint ne'er seen a hoss like this'n afor. Hit gots the narve an the blood."

Both finished applying saddle and bridle in silence.

Once all done Davy faced Matt. "Right, then. Have you and your brother decided about my offer on your mountain?"

"Yessir. Shore have."

Now Jack Davy was on his thoroughbred cantering away from Matt's cabin.

Matt and Cindy were helping Jimmie put apples into a wash pan under the apple tree.

Matt's freshly washed and brushed filly trotted around from behind his cabin, head and tail high, and followed Jack and his horse a little ways from the cabin.

Jack's horse looked back at her.

Jack pulled on reins to straighten his head and spurred him. "Giddup! Let's get out of here!"

8

The Silver Dagger

Tom Cline had been up all night. He was tired, but he was smiling. He had not been hunting as he had told his wife Ellen. Well, not four-legged critters, anyway.

The very early sunlight was turning the clouds overhead bright orange with deep purple convolutions. Ole Tom thought to himself, *Red sky in mornin, sailor take warnin*, and chuckled. He also figured it was still too early for Ellen and Katy to be up, so he had to be quiet as he crept into the cabin. He set about thinking through all the things he needed to do before that to make all appear as though he had just arrived from an unsuccessful hunting trip. He'd have to include a surly attitude.

He reached the top of a rise in the road that afforded him the first sight of his cabin. "Dadburnit."

Light radiated through the windows on each side of the door. Smoke boiled out of the chimney.

"She has the far a-roarin an ever lamp lit." He had never seen this before. He reined in his horse to a stop and watched the cabin for a while. "Sumthin air set catawampus up yander." Ellen might be sick or hurt. Even worse, Katy might be sick or hurt. He heeled his horse to a gallop right up to the front door, dismounted and rushed right into the cabin.

Tom found Ellen provoking the coal fire with a poker whose tip was glowing bright red. Although she was soaking wet with sweat, she seemed fine. Tom did not see Katy. "What kinder doins air this; whar be Katy!?"

Ellen twirled around to face Tom and pointed the poker at him. "Katy air at Lucy Lee's. Whar ye bin!?"

The poker made Tom forget about that surly attitude. He took a short moment to compose himself. "Out huntin fer yore vittles! As I tole yer!"

"With Tillman Brand, as ye tole me!?"

"Right!"

"Wrong! I saw Millie at the settlemint yestiddy afternoon. She tole me Tillman was home ailin!" Ellen emphasized that last word with an upward snap of the poker.

"As ye say! I dint go with Tillman! Wunst I larnt he was ailin, I set out on my own!" Tom added, "I went ter Grover's ter see if he could go, but he said he had ter re-place a wheel on his wagon."

"Grover, eh? Well, Millie rode ter the settlemint with Daisy in that thar wagon. It had all four wheels when I saw it!"

"Reckon he fixed it sooner'n he figgered!"

Ellen took a step toward Tom with the poker aimed right at his face. In complete control of her voice now she said, "Tell me bout Sally." Ellen saw Tom's eyes dilate.

After a pause and a swallow Tom asked, "Sally who?"

Ellen took another step toward Tom. "Sally Goodin fum Clairfiel'!" She took another step. "Sally what come inter Eli's store yestiddy a-lookin fer 'John Hardy!'" She took another step. "'John Hardy' what stans six foot an more, wit a smooth, broad jaw, thick, wavy yaller har, an piercin green eyes! 'John Hardy' what wars the silvry-gray high-crowned hat wit the military coat button wit a number six sewed onter the ban!" Ellen saw Tom's green eyes dart upward toward his silvery-gray high-crowned hat, and she raised the poker up high and charged.

Tom ducked and raised his left hand. He caught Ellen's right wrist on her downswing.

The sudden stop caused Ellen to lose her grip on the poker. It left her hand and continued downward. The hot tip smacked Tom's backside, burned a hole clear through his brown jeans and union suit and reached bare skin before falling to the floor.

"Aaaaahh!" As Tom screamed he swung his right hand up and out, connecting squarely with Ellen's torso just below her sternum.

She staggered backward, lost her footing and landed hard on the floor against her big cedar chest.

Everyone stopped.

Ellen took a long moment to regain her breath.

Tom stood absolutely still, confounded and remorseful. He really did not mean to hit her so hard. The excitement of their argument, his pain and his self-defense reflex added more to his blow than he intended. The spectacle of his wife sprawled on the floor, slammed against the chest, trying hard to breathe normally, made him lose all ability to move.

Ellen moved first. She struggled up and struggled more to push up the lid to the chest. She bent in deep and rummaged briefly. She emerged and turned holding a giant dagger. It was her grandfather's dirk. He had been a chieftain in Northumberland. He could afford an extravagantly ornate dirk with a silver wire handle. She let the lid fall and she fell back onto it. She withdrew the dirk from its scabbard and pointed it at Tom. All the stories her mother had told her of her life in northern England rushed in. How they were revered and loved by their clansmen. Now memories of Tom's routine infidelity crowded all those out.

"Ye caint e'en begin ter know how hoomiliated I was when this purty lil Sally come inter Eli's an started askin whar ter find 'John Hardy.' Ever person in thar knew zactly who she was askin bout. The whole group jes stood thar lookin et me. No one. No one! Come ter my side. While this Sally was a-chatterin away, Eli was a-lookin at me, too. He had the ev'list smirk on his face."

Tom realized feeling had returned to his legs and he started to move toward Ellen and hold his arms out for a hug.

Ellen snapped the dirk up higher and out toward Tom's throat.

He stopped.

"This here air the las time. I stuck wit yer ever time ye dun this ter me afore. Sumtimes I'd think ye would change yore ways; I would be a better wife an ye would luv me more. Sumtimes I'd think it was all my fault; thar was sumthin I jes dint hev that all o these other gals did an I accepted that. Sumtimes I'd think Katy an me couldn' make out thout yer; we needed yer ter werk the craps an hunt fer us. Well, lil Miss Sally Goodin's dun put a right smart stop ter all o them notions."

Ellen was standing now and back in control of her breath. She took a step toward Tom with that big knife. In her normal everyday voice she said, "Git out. Git outter here rat now."

Tom shifted his weight to take a step toward her, but she jabbed the dirk in the air at his pants.

"Take what ye gots on yore back an leave. Mos' probly Katy an me'll die o hunger. But that air more desire'ble than eatin the shame ye sarve up constantly. After we air daid ye kin have this place all ter yersef, an all the gals ye want."

Tom still wasn't getting the hint.

"Now! Now! Now!" Ellen emphasized each word with a swipe of the dirk.

Tom decided a burn on the butt was all he could tolerate that day. He didn't fancy cuts on the hands or elsewhere. "Okay! If that air what ye really want! I air a-goin! An jes as ye say I aint a-comin back till ye an Katy air both daid!" Tom did choke a little when he said that, because he did kind of love Ellen and he truly loved his daughter Katy. He took a quick glance behind him to locate the door and backed out of the cabin. He mounted up and rode off.

It was about three in the afternoon and Katy Cline was nigh well spent. Up before daylight to milk the cow. Over to the coop to gather a few eggs. Back to the cabin to eat some for breakfast. Out to the barn to bridle the mule and lead him out to the pasture.

Ellen had been right by her side helping until mid-morning when she went in to fix dinner. After they had eaten and cleaned up Ellen said, "Katy dear, I air feelin mighty peak-ed. I air minded ter lay down fer a spell."

"Awright, Maw. They aint much needs doin terday. I kin do it."

"Thank ee, chile. Thank ee."

This had become pretty routine. They'd both work like dogs for half a day. Then Ellen would go lie down after lunch for the rest of the day. Whatever needed doing that afternoon, Katy did it. Hauling water. Chopping firewood. Hoeing the garden. Plowing the field. Harvesting the crop. Then scraping together some leftovers for supper. But, they were surviving. They weren't going to die of starvation.

Presently, Katy was out front washing clothes. This was a tricky process of keeping the water in the cast iron pot hot enough, but not too hot, and stirring the clothes in the water mixed with enough lye soap, but not too much. Many chances to burn fingers. She was intent on adding little bits of wood to the fire under the pot when she thought she heard someone down the road. She stood up and looked in that direction.

Someone was singing.

"Roaming with thee I am happy and free,
Dreaming of thee fills my heart full of glee,
Longing for thee brings a sad memory
Sweet little maid of the mountain."

Katy recognized the voice. Her face flushed. Her heart jumped and started beating faster. She looked down at the pot of clothes and then over at the cabin door and then back down the road. She started running toward his voice.

Willie Moore came into view and Katy's heart leaped again. She looked again back at the cabin and then back at Willie, who by then was just yards away. "Quit that sangin! Ye'll wake my mam!"

Willie reined in his horse. "Hello, Katy dear. Why? It's a beautiful day and you are a beautiful girl well worthy of a song!" Willie didn't talk in the vernacular Katy did. His family was originally from the Midwest. His mother home schooled him.

"Quit talkin like that. Why air ye here?"

"Why do I grieve when I'm left alone? Why do I sigh when thou art gone?" He sang again.

"Please, Willie. Please!"

Willie decided Katy was serious. He frowned. "What's the matter? I came all this way just to visit you, and you are angry at me. What did I do?"

Katy closed her eyes and took a deep breath. It took a moment to calm down. "I aint angry at yer. Ye jes aint a-lissenin. I tole yer afore. I aint intersted. I aint merryin nobody. I saw how my pap treated my mam an my mam tells me all men air jes the same. They all sweet talk yer an lie ter yore face with the very next breath. I aint gonter have the same thang happin ter me. I has decided ter remain sangle all my life."

"Katy! You know I aint . . . "

"Stop! Makes no difference what I think nohow. My mam warns me she'll top off any man what e'en looks at me ser'ous. An ter remine me o that she carries that thar big silver dagger o hern with her migh nigh ever day."

"I don't believe she'd do any such thing. That's crazy talk." Willie had one more thought but a scream from inside the cabin chased it away.

"Katy? Katy! Who ye talkin ter out thar!? Air it a man come ter court yer? I air a-comin out thar rat now! I air a-comin wit my dagger!"

"No, Maw! No call ter come out! It air jes a feller what loss his way. He air leavin! Leavin rat now!" As she talked Katy pushed on Willie's horse's neck. To Willie she said, "Git on away from here! Now! An quit tryin me! I aint intersted I say. Maw aint gonter 'low sech nohow."

Willie watched her from his saddle. What he was seeing and hearing just didn't make any sense.

Katy was getting desperate. She slapped the poor horse's neck several times hard with both hands. She grabbed its reins and dragged horse and rider around to face the direction from whence they had come. She wiped her nose with her forearm. "Go, Willie. Ye caint come roun here no more. Caint e'en speak ter me no more. Go an find yesef sum other gal ter court stead o me."

Willie relented. "All right, Katy. You can let go of my horse now. I reckon this is good bye. Forever."

Katy released the reins and stepped back.

Willie took up the slack and looked down at the red-faced mountain maid looking up at him for what he thought would be the last time.

She bolted up the hill toward her cabin with a hand over her nose and mouth.

Willie watched her enter. He watched the wash pot bubble over and splash the fire underneath. He watched the steam rise and evaporate. Then he bade his horse carry him home, pulled out his handkerchief and wiped his wet eyes.

Willie and James Moore started out in the elder's buckboard from their house on the hill up above the coal camp. They headed toward the settlement and Eli Parch's Mercantile.

"You got Ma's list?" The elder asked.

Willie tapped his chest. "Yessir." He pulled the list out and looked at it. It included measurements for a new suit for him. The night before at supper he, his dad, and his mom talked about him going to college in Knoxville to study business.

Sitting beside his dad for the trip to Eli's was the typical awkward event between son and father. Conversation was sporadic, short and on general topics. Weather. Work. Despite all that, Willie was feeling pretty good. The sky was absolutely clear. The mid-morning sun was warm. He had forgotten his last visit with Katy.

At last they arrived. A teamster's wagon fastened to two mules stood idle around to the side of the store.

Across the road the sound of hammered steel echoed through the open doors of Charlie Waggoner's smithy.

A skinny little boy with thin ragged clothes, sitting on a barrel beside the doors waved.

James parked directly in front of the steps up to Eli's front porch, nudging away a mule at the rail beside the steps.

"Careful, Dad."

James just chuckled and hopped down. "Let's get you ready for college." James took the steps two at a time and Willie followed suit.

Just inside James asked for the list, took it and went straight for Eli just ringing out a customer. "Eli, help me with this list."

"Yessir, Mr. Moore. Right away." To his current customer he said, "Thank ee, Miss Cline. Say hey ter yore mam."

Heretofore, after he had given the list to his dad, Willie had wandered to the back of the store to look at a display of fishing flies. When he heard "Cline" he felt the hair on the back of his neck stand up like the hair on the shanks of the flies. He turned around. He saw Katy turn to leave and face his father. Her face was crimson. He saw her look down at the floor. He barely heard her say, "Scuse me, sir."

She turned to walk around James and looked into the depths of the store, spying Willie. Capillaries around her brain tightened. She stopped briefly to concentrate on not fainting then ran out the front door.

Eli and James watched her peculiar behavior mildly curious, then turned back to business.

Willie watched Katy's peculiar behavior with great interest, watched his dad and Mr. Parch discussing the list, then scurried out the door.

Outside, he saw Katy running away. He called, "Katy! Stop a minute. Can't I at least say hello?"

"No!" She did not slow down.

Willie caught up and grabbed her arm.

She turned and swung her free hand at him.

He ducked and let her go.

Both looked at each other a little breathless, unsure of why they were breathless. Breathing for both normalized but they still said nothing. They just looked at each other.

Finally Katy closed her eyes. "No. No. No. Ye caint be trusted. No man kin. If ye air so all fired consarned, I air fine. I air happy.

Maw and me air doin tolerble fine on our own." She whipped around and headed up the road. "She air a-waitin fer me."

Willie prepared to follow her but his father's voice behind him commanded his immediate attention.

"Willie! Leave that gal alone and come back here! You gotta choose a color for your suit! … Now, Willie!"

"Yessir." Willie went back to the store a lot slower than he had left.

"Who was that, anyway? You looked mighty interested."

"Uh, Katy Cline. Lives with her mom between here and Arthur."

"What's her daddy do?"

"Don't know. He aint around."

"So, just the two of em? How they gettin on?"

"Just gardenin. Some huntin I reckon. A little cash crop."

"Well, that's pretty sad, but you don't need to be gettin mixed up with all that. You got your own life to prepare for. You sure can't be wastin your time and energy on some dirt poor gal from around here. She looked okay from where I could see. Plenty a boys in these hills will be followin her around soon enough. Those city gals in Knoxville will make you forget her in a hurry. Get inside and tell Mr. Parch what to order for ya … Ya hear? … Willie!"

Willie was watching Katy disappear into the woods at a bend in the road. "Why do I grieve when I'm left alone?"

"What? … Get inside!"

"Yessir."

"Willie? … Willie!"

He was upstairs reading when his mother started calling. "Yes, Mother?"

"This little boy says your suit is in at Mr. Parch's. Why don't you ride in and pick it up?"

To himself. *Ah, a good excuse to get out of this stuffy house. Maybe a good hard ride will make me feel better.* To his mother, "Yes'm!" He hopped out of his bed and went straightaway downstairs.

103

At the foot he found his mother and the little boy who had waved at him from the blacksmith's a month ago. His mother was giving him a quarter. The boy was acting as though he was getting a hundred dollars.

To his mom, "I'll saddle up and be on my way." To the boy, "How'd you get here? You need a ride back?"

The boy smiled wider than any youngster Willie had ever seen. "Nawsir! Thank ee. I gots my mule!" The boy pointed out toward the front yard to an ancient swayback critter that was dustier than the kid. The kid ran out to the animal, executed an impressive leap up onto its back and shook the reins.

The mule ambled off with his proud master.

Willie ran out to the barn, set up his own ride, aimed it toward the settlement and heeled it as hard as he could.

"That all there is?" Willie asked Eli.

"Yessir. The whole lay out."

"Hum. Thought it would be a bigger box than that." Willie took off the lid.

"Reglar size wool tree piece suit. Blue pin stripe. A timeless standard." Eli recited the copy from the catalogue.

Willie put the lid back on. "Anything else for us?"

"Naw. S'everthink."

"Hum. Okay then."

"Aint ye wantin ter try it on? S'common fer these here mail order suits ter need sum alteration ter fit proper. Be happy ter do that fer ye. Jes a dollar."

"Um. Can I come back with it later?"

"Why, a course ye kin. Ennytime."

"Thanks." Willie was underwhelmed. His parents' talk and arrangements over his trip in the fall to college had been incessant and infectious. Naturally, he was excited in his own right. College— the big city—away from parents for the first time in his life. Everyone's expectations were high. This plain brown box, containing a symbol of a timeless standard life, brought him back down to earth fast and hard. He remembered the honest joy the little messenger got out of a mere quarter, and the pride he had for his worn-out mule. He turned away from Eli and headed for the door. "Gotta go."

"Preciate yore bizness. Give my best ter yore mam and pap."

Willie heard only the first half of this. By the time Eli had finished his farewell, he was on his horse and headed toward Arthur.

The oddest feelings overcame the boy. He could see things quite clearly; the clouds above him; the trees around him; his horse underneath him. And they were indeed moving along this wagon trail. Yet there was some sensation swirling around him that was invisible yet palpable. It made vision and forward movement seem to require prodigious effort. It was as if the atmosphere were three times as dense as water. Willie didn't know to call it depression. He just thought it was the byproduct of the colossal conflict engaging his entire being.

One force drove him forward to Katy's cabin, arguing he absolutely must see her again.

The other force held him back, arguing her mother would kill him, and maybe Katy, too. At the very least she would cause a whole lot of distress and anxiety in everyone.

Eventually the force holding him back prevailed. Much as he wanted to see her, he wanted to upset her less. He stopped his horse. He remained in place for a minute. He turned around and headed home.

He took a more direct route to his house. That brought him to a stream. He followed it a ways downstream looking for a decent ford.

For the most part it flowed straight and swiftly downhill over polished rocks and deadfall. At one point it entered a flat spot, slowed and bent, creating a broad, level bank along its concave side. The bank had grass and trees and Katy.

Willie pulled in hard and stared. There was definitely a girl in there. She was sitting on a rock right next to the stream fishing. Willie started back up slowly, not sure of what he was seeing. The closer he got the surer he became.

She heard someone approaching and turned. She stood and dropped her fishing pole half into the water. She watched him ride into the glade, dismount and stride right up to her. She held out her arms to welcome him, closed her eyes and lifted her face up to his. She felt his arms draw her body in tightly to his. She felt his mouth on hers. She felt all her sadness, confusion, and guilt vanish. She felt incalculable joy warm her entire body. She wanted to feel him inside her. She felt him pull her down onto the ground right where they had been standing.

"I air truly sorry fer the way I acted. I sot mesef with all my might ter fergit ye. I sot mesef with all my might ter foller my mam's way o thinkin. The more I tried the wurse I felt. ... What air we gonter do, Willie?"

"I was miserable. After you left Eli's I felt like my life had ended. All the talk about Knoxville helped some; but a little while ago when I got my suit, I looked in the box and saw only an endless dark pit. ... We're just gonna have to convince our folks. I reckon it'll be pretty hard. But, I aint gonna spend a whole lot a time'n energy tryin. If they don't come round then we'll just run away. I hear land farther down the Powell is practically free. We'll get us some and start our own life down there. ... Know what? My momma should be the first we talk to. I've seen how she can pretty much get her way with Daddy all the time. After that, we all can talk to your mom."

"Knoxvull!? What air ye talkin bout?"

"Oh, right. You wouldn't know bout that. They're sending me to college there to study business. Er, were plannin to send me there. I aint going now. I'm stayin here with you."

Despair found a chink in Katy's psyche. She sat up from where she was lying and straightened her clothes. As she did she said, "Knoxvull. Colletch." She got up and went down to her fishing pole. She picked it up and checked the hook. The worm was gone. She pulled another out of the tin can beside the rock and ran the

106

hook through it in several places. In the process she ran the point into her thumb. It hurt like the dickens. She said nothing. She swung the hooked worm out into a calm patch of water next to the downstream side of a log. As she watched the cork she said, "Ye gots ter go. Yer parents air doin sa much fer ye. S'a fust rate chance fer yer. Ye caint let that'n go. Go. I'll be fine." She took a real deep breath hoping to quell the surge of despair. Willie hugged her from behind and she started bawling.

"Stop cryin. Maybe Knoxville is the answer. You can come with me. We'll find work for you there. Point is, we'll be together. We'll figger things out. First things first. I gotta talk to Mom."

This made her feel better but only a little more so. She still watched the cork. "Right. Right. Fust thangs fust. Talk ter yore mam."

Willie kissed the top of her head. Then an ear. Then all around the back of her neck. Between each kiss he said, "I love you." He pressed his hand against one of her breasts. She dropped the pole, turned around and pressed both hard against his body. They went back up to where they had lain before.

After Willie had left her in the glade, Katy lingered on the grass, looking up through the trees, seeing forms of herself and Willie in the clouds. She replayed their time together over and over again in her mind. She touched the ground with her fingers. She had a persistent feeling she was floating. The sound of hoof beats behind her brought her back down. She rolled over onto her stomach and looked up toward the sound. "Willie?"

"Katy? It air yore paw, chile."

Katy rolled back onto her back and sat up facing away from Tom. She checked her clothing. She stood up and faced her father. "Paw? What air ye doin here?"

"Lookin fer you-uns."

"Ye dint go by the cabin?"

"No, no. I knows bettern that. I membered this was yore favo-rite spot ter git away fum thangs. I set out fer here fust." He dismounted and made to hug his daughter.

She backed up ever so slightly, but he noticed and stopped.
"I'd shore like ter set an talk."

"Reckon no harm thar." She went down to her fishing pole and
checked the hook. It was bare. She twirled the line around the pole
and leaned it on the rock beside her. She sat beside it.

Tom came up and sat on the ground in front of her. "I jes got
ter missin yer. I wanted ter know ye was fairin well."

"Fairin fine."

"Yer mam?"

"She's okay. ... Parful sad all the time."

"Reckon so."

"Ye dun er mighty wrong. Dun me mighty wrong. I thinks she
still luvs yer ennyways."

"I know. I know. I air hepless bout my ways. I see a gal I'd like
ter meet an one thang leads ...."

"Stop! I aint wantin ter hear bout sech thangs."

"Sorry. A course. Uh. How be the farm?"

"Huh. Okay. Maw an me air doin our bestes ter keep it runnin.
We air bout even. Made us sum money on the corn this yar."

"How bout you-uns? Got enny plans?"

"Well, I was a-thinkin I had plans. They jes got all turned roun.
Don' rightly know what's ter happen, now."

"What? Tell me. Mebbe I kin hep."

"I met me a boy. Since ye bin gone, I bin countin on stayin
sangle all er my life. Maw heps by reminin me right offen bout yore
doins. An I was doin good till I met him. I tried ter fight it. But, I
dun loss that battle." She looked back up to the place where they
had lain.

"Ah, that thar air fust rate news! I air sa happy fer yer! Don'
lissin ter yore mam bout this. Mos' men aint a-kin ter me. Mos' men
air true ter their wimmen. Sides, ye gots ter make up yore own mine
bout sech thangs after seein em fer yesef. Don' 'low yore mam ter
decide yore life fer yer. Tell me bout yore boy."

"Fust saw im at the train wreck a while back." Saw im werkin ter clar them tracks. Took no break cept ter drank sum water when someone offered it ter im. Then after everthink was clared off an them tracks were set ter rights we was eatin an I saw im watchin me. I saw he was took with me, too. He jes looked right back at me an ne'er turned way. He jes smiled, an bowed. … One day he came a-callin an was sangin this be-ootiful luv song." Katy noticed Tom shift.

"Huh. Bowin an sangin. That air odd behav'or fer roun hyar. He with that thar Ainglish feller what air a-buyin lan' fer the coal compny?"

"Naw, but his pap air a-werkin fer the mine. I reckon he gots a tad more larnin than mos' folks roun here."

Tom stood up. He paced around in a circle. He took his silver-grey hat off and scratched his head. As he paced and scratched he said, "This aint gonter do. Jes aint gonter do."

"What air ailin yer, paw?"

"You-uns! Took up wit the coal bizness! Ye caint be merryin inter that! They air rapin the lan'! Cuttin the innards outer the mountins an tarnin their outsides black all at wunst! An them miners! Ne'er seein the light er day. Tarnin their blood black! Livin in pov'ty. Slaves ter the owners wit their compny stores an scrip!"

"Paw! Ye caint do this ter me! What was it ye was jes a-sayin!? Bout makin up my own mine!?" Her father's self-righteousness about anything was as equally as startling as his reversal on her judgment.

"Ye oughter be takin more pride in yore home. Take keer o yore famly an the lan' fust. Them mines air de-stroyin everthink. No, Katy. I aint a-gonter bless that oon'on. Matter o fact, whar kin I fine this boy? I air wantin ter have a word." At this Tom grabbed the haft of his Arkansas Toothpick and pulled it halfway out of its sheath stuck in the belt of his pants.

The sight of this shut Katy down completely. The loud rushing of thousands of thoughts through her mind confounded her. She couldn't speak. She just sat there looking down at the grass, then at the quiet spot of water she had fished, then back to Tom. "Wha? … Wha?"

Tom mounted his horse. "I gots ter go. I air meetin .... But, mine ye, lil gal, I air a-watchin yer." He rode off.

Katy slid down and sat on the ground, back and head against the rock. She wanted to see the cloud forms of her and Willie again but she could focus on nothing but the branches of the trees, that now seemed to be reaching down to strangle her. Now tears blurred everything.

Anne Moore stood there a moment with her left hand cupping her chin and her right arm against her tummy supporting her left. She walked slowly around in a circle studying Willie, who was standing on a low stool wearing his brand new blue pin stripe three-piece suit. This went on a whole lot longer than Willie thought it should. Finally his mom said, "It looks perfect to me. Fits you just right. You'll be the handsomest young man in Knoxville."

Willie felt a whole lot of heat rise from the bottom of his neck up through the top of his head. He looked down and around him at his suit. It did look good. An image of him strutting down a city street with it on flashed into his mind. An image of Katy lying on the grass looking up at him with her hair spread out on the grass like a halo overwhelmed that one. He started to tell his mother about her then, but his throat tightened up considerably. He elected to try later.

That night at supper his father was pretty agitated about work. As best as Willie could understand, too many miners were coming in sick, or hung over, or something. Production was too far below quotas.

"They're holding me responsible, dontcha know! Me! Do they expect me to go out personally and axe the still!? ... Anne, what have you been doing all day!? Not tending to this meal, that's for sure! I might understand if you had spent the day cleaning the house!"

Willie saw his mom's eyes lower and her cheeks redden and elected to talk to her later.

The next morning he heard voices downstairs. He recognized the voices of some of the women from the coal camp. They would occasionally come and bring Anne some vegetables from their gardens. The visits were always short and awkward but always put Anne in an outstanding mood. He descended the staircase as they were saying their goodbyes. He picked up two of the baskets and carried them into the kitchen.

Anne followed with the other two and a gratified look on her face. Now.

"Mom, I've met someone. A girl. I first noticed her after the train wreck, when everyone was eating and resting after cleaning up. I ...."

That was as much as Willie got out before his mother grabbed him, spun him around and hugged him harder than he ever remembered her hugging him before. "Oh, Willie! What good news! Wonderful news! I can't wait to meet her! Your pa will be happy, too, I know it! We been talking about that. Er. Oh! There's college! Does she know about that? No matter! We'll figure something out. I just know it! When can I meet her?"

"Well. Today. Maybe. If you don't have other plans."

"No. No plans. Other than cleaning the house." Anne laughed out loud.

It took a moment, but then Willie laughed out loud with her.

"Oh. The party. That'll be the perfect time for everyone to meet her and her folks."

"Party?"

"Of, course. Your going away party. You can invite her and her parents."

"Well. Uh. Her parents are, uh, separated."

"Oh, that's too bad. Do you think they'd mind if her father came, too? Your dad will insist on meeting him at some point."

"No. I mean, yes. I think they would mind. They didn't split on good terms. I don't think they even know where he is."

"Well, Dad absolutely must meet him. Me, too. What's his name? Dad will know someone who can find him."

Willie took a moment. "Tom Cline. I think its Tom. I ... I'm not sure. I never met him."

"Tom Cline. That name sounds familiar. Where do they live?"

"They, well, Katy and her mom, have a farm just off the road to Arthur."

"Katy. I like that name. A farm? They're farmers? I'm sorry. I just assumed they were in the business. How many acres?"

"Oh, forty. I guess."

"Forty? Willie, that's nearly nothing. They can't be doing well."

"Well, no. They aren't doing well at all. Just the two of them."

"Cline. Tom Cline. What's the mother's name?"

Willie felt a little constriction in his throat. "Ellen."

Willie had good reason to feel uncomfortable.

Anne stood there looking at him and frowning. Then her eyes widened and she declared, "Tom and Ellen Cline!? Tom and Ellen Cline!? Oh, Willie, how could you!? How would you even meet people like that?"

"I, I told you I met her at the train wreck."

As Willie was talking his mother continued. "The women from the coal camp told me all about them last time they were here! The man is a womanizer of the worst sort! Absolutely shameless about his behavior! The woman is crazy! Keeps some huge butcher knife or something with her all the time! Raves about killin anybody that even looks at the girl! And poor! They don't have more'n twenty acres! Can't tend to even that much! Willie, you can not; you will not, associate with those people! They are a sad, crazy, hopeless family! Can't sort themselves out enough to take care of themselves!"

Willie was not there. A throbbing buzzing had developed in his head. Halfway through his mother's rant while she scrubbed vegetables, he had backed out of the kitchen and had run out the front door down to the barn. He now leaned against a wall. His racing heart, throbbing head and stinging eyes overpowered him. He

112

bent down and put his hands on his knees. He was pretty sure he was going to vomit.

He breathed deeply, swallowed repeatedly and planned what to do. He liked the plan and that calmed him down a little. He went back up to the house.

"Willie!? Where'd you go?"

"Just outside."

"You hear me about those Cline people?"

"Yes, ma'am."

"You gonna break it off with that girl?"

His throat got tight. His answer squeaked out. "Yes, ma'am." He coughed. "Thought I'd go do that now." He was half way up the stairs.

"Good boy. I'm sorry, son. There'll be another one soon enough. Plenty of the right kind of girls for you in Knoxville."

He was in his room by then, stuffing clothes into a suitcase.

Completing that he snuck halfway down the stairs, looked and listened for his mother. He could hear her in the kitchen singing while she swept the floor. He snuck back up to the top of the stairs, grabbed his suitcase and snuck back down and out the front door. Off the porch, he ran to the barn.

Willie galloped right up to Ellen, who was out in front of her cabin washing clothes. "Where's Katy!?"

"Inside! In bed! Took ill two days ago! I gots ter do all the werk roun here! ... Who air ye, comin roun here axin bout Katy!? Ye aint got no bizness here!"

"I. I'm. I'm here to take her away! Away from you and your crazy notions!"

"I knew it! Jes knew she'd met someone. She bin actin pecul'ar fer weeks now. Chillen these days. Aint got no sef control. I gots ter step in. Get outer here! Leave us be! She aint runnin off wit you-uns! Nobody! She aint gonter git hart like her mam!"

"I aint nothin like her pa! I love her!"

Ellen ran into the cabin. Almost instantly she was back outside screaming. "She's gone! Its gone!"

Willie twisted his horse's neck double to turn it. It shrieked but took off. He could hear Ellen shrieking behind him as he galloped toward the glade.

Katy was there. She was on her knees on the spot where they had lain together. She was pulling the silver dagger out of its sheath.

The atmosphere again became thrice as dense as water.

Now Katy held the dirk up with both hands, with its point aimed at her chest.

Willie was off his horse running toward her. He made no headway through the super dense air.

The point of the dirk was against her skin.

"KATY!!" Willie heard himself screaming, but just could not tell if any sound was coming out of his mouth.

Katy did not turn. She looked up into the sky. She pressed.

The tip of the dirk entered her breast.

"Katy! Katy! Katy! Katy!"

The dirk was halfway into her chest.

Willie dropped to his knees in front of her and grabbed her arms.

She looked at him from marveling at the ornate handle. "Goodbye, Mamma. Goodbye, Papa. I die for the one I love the best."

Willie was left holding up a lifeless body. He gently laid it on its side. He placed its hands together and tucked them under its head. He caressed its hair. He became aware that the dirk was now half buried in his own chest. He lay on his side and snugged up against Katy's back. That pushed the dirk all the way in. "Farewell Mamma; farewell Daddy. I follow the one that I would wed."

Ellen Cline, running on foot all the way from her cabin, found them lying together. She saw both on their sides. His body was tight against her back. His arm was draped over her side. His face was nestled in her hair. She sprinted down to them enraged. Their backs were to her; so, it was not until she was directly over them that she saw all the blood.

In the chapel in the dale, on the right side of the center aisle, James and Anne Moore sat in the front row pew. Her parents sat beside her and his parents sat beside him. Their brothers and sisters, nieces and nephews filled the two rows behind them. More distant relatives, friends and business associates filled all the rows behind them.

Ellen Cline sat on the front row on the left side of the aisle. Lucy Lee Reilly sat next to her, holding her hand. Lucy Lee's father Louvin Reilly sat beside her. Ellen's brothers and sisters, nieces and nephews sat in the next two rows behind her. Tom Cline's relatives sat in rows behind them. Friends of both and of Katy's filled all the rows behind them. Tom sat in the very last row, at the end closest to the door.

All listened to Parson Brown up front behind a small podium saying the strangest things for a funeral.

"Our Father, love has been Your richest and greatest gift to the world. Love between a man and woman is one of Your most beautiful types of loves. Today we celebrate that love. May your blessing be upon this service for Katy and Willie. Surround them and us with Your love now and always.

We give thanks for the nurture and support of family and friends. Let us who share the circle of celebration today be renewed in our own commitments to one another that we may participate in a healed and healing society."

Between the congregation and the parson was a rosewood casket. It was likewise unusual for a funeral. It was half again as wide as normal.

9

Cumberland Gap

Ever since it was built many years ago the little church in the dale had never been painted. The new circuit rider who had made it his headquarters a few months ago had asked for donations from everyone at every community he served to paint it. He was thoroughly disappointed by the response. Then, out of the blue, a major donor come through.

Monday morning a week ago had been particularly trying for Parson Jeremy Brown and his wife Eleanor. They were both up extra early. They both had to ready him for a week of travel. He had just conducted his first two funerals. He was facing his second wedding. He couldn't find his notes on the sermons he had planned for that week.

She had to ready herself for a week of teaching school at the church. Her horse was acting colicky.

Once on the way they rode together to the church in sullen silence. They rounded the bend in the road that afforded a person the first view of the church. They simultaneously reined in. They saw a dozen African Americans wearing black and white striped clothes on several ladders painting the side of the church building.

Now instead of being a weathered brown, its exterior would be a shiny white.

Eleanor reached over and placed her hand over Jeremy's. Both bowed their heads and Jeremy spoke aloud a tender prayer of thanksgiving and forgiveness.

Now a small group of people dressed in their Sunday best clustered beside the church. It included Matthew Johnson's betrothed Cindy Grove, Mark Johnson's betrothed Katy Daly and Angeline Baker.

Louvin Reilly's daughter Lucy Lee was in their midst, wearing a simple white dress that rivaled the church in color and luster. She held a bouquet of wildflowers tied together with ribbons the color of lush green and rich purple. "I air ready now."

Angeline said, "I'll go an tell the music'ans ter start. Ye look be-ootiful."

Inside the church, bunches of mountain laurel and lighted candles graced the sills of the big windows along its sides. Lucy Lee Reilly and her soon-to-be husband John Behan stood up front facing Parson Jeremy Brown. Cindy and Katy stood by her left side. Matt and Mark Johnson stood by John's right.

Louvin Reilly sat on the front row on the left side. Angeline sat with him, holding his hand in her lap.

Behind them a large contingent of the community sat in the pews hewn by the hands of parishioners from generations ago.

With the voice of a novice professional eager to impress his new flock, Parson Brown declared, "I now pronounce you man and wife. You may kiss the bride!"

John obeyed. He obeyed for exactly one minute.

Once he broke for air, everyone stood and clapped.

Mr. and Mrs. Behan turned and walked down the aisle.

A woman played a recessional on a concertina, accompanied by a very old man playing a fiddle.

The Behans exited the chapel and everyone inside cheered.

Ribbons and greenery adorned the door of Bill Vaughn's barn. In the front yard a pile of wood burned inside a rock fire ring. A swarthy man with bushy white hair and beard wearing leather clothes polkaed with a goat to the tune of "Soldier's Joy" emanating from inside the barn. They sashayed dangerously close to the fire.

The inside of Bill's barn was similarly decorated. Chairs were clustered here and there. On one wall was a long table made with boards on saw horses. It was loaded with food, drink and a fancy wedding cake, about half of which had been cut away. Slices on small plates surrounded it.

Everyone who had been at the church earlier were now here eating, talking and laughing with each other.

Little Jimmie Brown sat on a chair against a wall. He and his clothes were freshly washed. He shared a plate of fried chicken wings with his mom sitting next to him.

Johnny Oxford's mom sat with two other women about her age, eating, talking and smiling.

Jimmy Randall stood alone leaning against a wall with his arms crossed. He watched the festivities and smiled a little. Every once in a while he would look down at the spot where he had earlier laid Polly.

Eventually Katy Daly's big sister Corey came over and distracted him with a plate of food.

At the table Maggie Daly offered Eleanor Brown some punch.

Wanting very much to be accepted by the community, Eleanor took the cup and sipped the contents. "Mmmm." She got more, called her husband over and offered it to him.

He shook his head.

She kept holding the cup out in front of him, nodding.

He finally took it and sipped. He chugged the rest. "This is delicious!"

"Ol' fam'ly recipe." Maggie looked over at Donal, who was sitting on a small cask eating a piece of wedding cake. They both winked and smiled at each other.

At the opposite wall was a small platform on which Matt and Mark played their instruments. They were backing up the old man and woman musicians from the church. It was they who played "Soldier's Joy."

Katy and Cindy sat together on the floor against the platform looking up at their beaus.

The musicians ended that tune and went straight into "Boston Boy."

In the middle of the barn four couples stepped their way through a set dance.

The Justice of the Peace, Squire Harold Bateman, danced with a woman of similar age. As they moved close to Bill and Peggy Vaughn dancing together Bateman called, "Bill, Peg, fust rate shindig, as usual!"

Peggy dipped a little curtsey without breaking the beat. "Why, thank ee, Squire."

The Vaughns spun away toward Louvin and Angeline and traded partners.

Eli Parch and a woman of similar age danced toward Bill and Angeline. Parch's partner called to Angeline. "Be-ootiful cake, Angeline."

"Thank ee, Sare Jane."

The merriment continued through several more tunes.

The musicians started "Jenny Lynn."

After the first round everyone realized that Matt and the old fiddle player were sawing out a virtuoso duet performance. Mark and the concertina player had stopped playing. Everyone else stopped whatever they were doing to appreciate the two fiddlers.

Halfway through Part B of the fourth round the old fiddle player raised his right knee and both men ended the song with their own unique flourish.

Everyone took a moment to savor every last vestige of tonal vibration then applauded, whistled and cheered.

All the band members bowed.

Matt and the old fiddle player shook hands but realized that wasn't enough. They hugged.

Once they broke, the old fiddle player faced the crowd and stretched out his arms with his fiddle and bow in hand. "Well folks. It air time fer me ter go." Everyone clapped, cheered and whistled again.

He bowed deeply, arms outstretched. He turned, hung the fiddle and bow on pegs in the wall behind him, stepped off the platform and headed toward the door. He weaved through the crowd greeting a few people as he went amidst more clapping and cheering. He finally reached the door and stopped dead still. He backed up to allow Claiborne County Sheriff A. C. Hughes in.

All merriment ceased.

Jimmie Brown spied a mouse scampering away.

Everyone standing eased backward farther into the interior of the barn, leaving Louvin and Angeline standing alone in the middle of the dance area to face the Sheriff.

Sheriff Hughes gazed at the crowd in the back of the barn and touched the brim of his hat. "Shore air sorry ter de-sturb yore party, but I gots ter have a word wit Luvin an it jes caint wait." He focused on Louvin. "Constable Reilly?"

"Yessir?"

"'Pears ter me like this here corner o Clay-burn County has gonter hell in a handcart."

"Yessir."

"Trains a-wreckin. Younguns a-killin younguns. Miners a-riotin. Moonshine a-flowin like the Powell." Hughes cut his eyes briefly from Louvin to Donal and back.

Donal studied the tines of the fork he had been eating cake with.

Louvin studied Hughes's eyes. "Yessir."

"I come here ter night ter take yore badge."

Everyone in the back gasped. Several moved forward toward Louvin.

Angeline got up close to Louvin and hugged his arm. Her cheeks flushed and her jaw muscles gyrated. She took a deep breath to speak but Louvin broke in.

He squeezed her hand and said, "Git easy, Angeline. Sheriff's words air true. I bin thinkin bout quittin ennyways." Louvin set about unfastening the badge on his shirt. His hands wavered. Once it was off he looked down at it a moment then handed it to the Sheriff.

The Sheriff held it up high for everyone to see. "As I was a-sayin, life roun here took a parful bad turn. Mor'n mos' folkses sees in a lifetime. But don' look at Luvin as the problem. Naw, sir. All through this misry I seen im as re-sourceful, e'en-handed an kine ter all consarned. I reckon this whole commun'ty would a faired much wurse if Luvin warnt here a-hannelin thangs."

Hughes saw everyone relax a little but remain silent. He pulled a little box out of an inside pocket of his duster with his other hand. He held that up for everyone to see then gave it to Louvin. "Luvin, on be-haff er mesef an Clay-burn County, here air a token o our 'preciation. Ye bin a mighty toler'ble gov-mint sarvint. Stead o a badge war this fum here on out."

Louvin took the box. His hands shook even more as he pulled off the lid. He removed and held up a gold railroad watch for everyone to see.

Everyone in back finally found their voices. They cheered and shouted Louvin's name. They encircled him, Angeline and Hughes. They grabbed both men's hands and shook them. They hugged and kissed Angeline.

Three ushered the Sheriff over to the food table and piled a plate full of food for him.

He kept shaking his head and politely declining all the while shoveling vittles into his mouth.

The concertina player pushed out "For He's A Jolly Good Fellow" and Matt and Mark did a tolerable job of following.

The party cranked back up again.

As Hughes continued to enjoy the fare, Squire Bateman came alongside and started talking into his ear. Hughes raised his eyebrows and nodded.

Once the next song ended, he waved his hands and bade everyone get still and quiet again. "I air a-lookin ter re-place Luvin. One feller already come ter Tazewell an a-pplied. We sat an talked. I was 'fraid he'd be the only applycant. Now Squire Bateman here tells me I oughter be lookin at Mark Johnson." He nodded in Mark's direction.

Donal Daly laughed out loud.

Hughes looked back at him.

Donal's cheeks caught up with the color of his nose and he helped himself to more punch.

Hughes looked back at Mark with an inquiring expression.

Mark forwarded that inquiry on to Katy.

She nodded.

He looked over at Donal with a face a law enforcement officer might use with a minor miscreant.

Donal looked around the crowd and back at Mark. He nodded, too.

Mark turned back to Sheriff Hughes. "Thank ee kindly, Sheriff. An Squire. An everone. I air mighty proud ter do it."

Now everyone cheered and called out Mark's name. Many converged on him and Katy and exchanged handshakes, hugs and pecks on the cheek.

The cheeky concertina player played a fanfare.

Hughes said, "Thank ee, Mark. Come down ter Tazewell soon's yer kin. I gots ter swar yer in. Thank ee all; and thank ee agin, Luvin. I gots ter put out fer home." With that he headed for the door of the barn, carried along by more cheering.

At the door he met the mountain man coming in. The hem of one of the man's trouser legs was charred and smoking. They traded silent acknowledgments as the Sheriff disappeared into the night outside.

. . .

Louvin stood alone looking down at a grave stone inscribed, "Lorena Reilly, 1840-1883." He laid at its base a bunch of the same kind of flowers Lucy had had in her bouquet. "John air a good man. He air doin tolerble well by Lucy. He air mighty de-termined ter larn ter werk that thar farm o ourn." He pulled a handkerchief from his back pocket and wiped his eyes. "I air still a-missin yer an I'll always luv yer." He looked up and watched Lorena's brother's sons Matthew and Mark Johnson for a few moments.

Mark wore the same badge and revolver Louvin used to carry.

Both were tidying up around two head stones sitting side by side. One was inscribed "Luke Johnson, 1827-1876," and the other was inscribed, "Ruth Johnson, 1830-1876." Both of them stood up straight and dusted off their hands. They looked around and stopped at Louvin. They walked over.

He greeted them. "I fretted in my mine fer quite a spell o'er what I thought was bestes fer yer long term. I know now you-uns made the right decis'on."

Matt stretched both arms up and out in front of him to call attention to the view. They stood in a small, very well-maintained cemetery. Nearby were three fresh graves. One was about twice as wide as the other two. Hard by the cemetery was the little white church.

Beyond the church the men could see the dale widen into a vista of fields, forest, hills, and mountains, all basking in an unseasonably warm but comfortable sun. They could see Pinnacle Mountain and the break alongside it people called Cumberland Gap.

Matt said, "My heart air in the Highlans."

The Songs

"The Oxford Tragedy"
English Folk Songs from the Southern Appalachians
Collected by Olive Dame Campbell and Cecil J. Sharp
Copyright 1917 by Olive Dame Campbell and Cecil J. Sharp
G. P. Putnam's Sons, New York
From Mary Wilson and Mrs. Townley, Kentucky, 1917

"Shooting of his Dear"
From Jane Gentry at Hot Springs North Carolina August 25, 1916
Campbell and Sharp

"Mollie Bawn"
American Ballads and Songs
Collected and edited by Louise Pound
Professor of the English Language University of Nebraska
Copyright 1922 by Charles Scribner's Sons
Charles Scribner's Sons, New York

"Silver Dagger"
Pound

"Katy Dear"
From Carrie Ford at Black Mountain, NC September 19, 1916
Campbell and Sharpe

"Cumberland Gap"
Copyright 2014 Patrick R. Watts

The Oxford Tragedy

Once I was a little tailor boy
About sixteen years of age;
My father hired me to a miller
That I might learn the trade.

I fell in love with a Knoxville girl,
Her name was Flora Dean.
Her rosy cheeks, her curly hair,
I really did admire.

Her father he persuaded me
To take Flora for a wife;
The devil he persuaded me
To take Flora's life.

Up stepped her mother so bold and gay,
So boldly she did stand;
Johnny dear, go marry her
And take her off my hands.

I went unto her father's house
About nine o'clock at night,
A-asking her to take a walk
To do some prively talk.

We had not got so very far
Till looking around and around,
I stooping down picked up a stick
And knocked little Flora down.

She fell upon her bended knees,
For mercy she did cry;
O Johnny dear, don't murder me,
For I'm not fit to die.

I took her by her lily-white hands
A-slung her around and around;
I drug her off to the river-side,
And plunged her in to drown.

I returned back to my miller's house
About nine o'clock at night,
But little did my miller know
What I had been about.

The miller turned around and about,
Said: "Johnny, what blooded your clothes?"
Me being so apt to take a hint:
By bleeding at the nose.

About nine or ten days after that,
Little Flora she was found
A-floating down by her father's house
Who lived in Knoxville town.

Shooting of His Dear

Jimmy Daniels went a-hunting
Between sunset and dark;
Her white apron over her shoulder,
He took her for a swan.

He throwed down his gun
And to her he run.
He hugged her, he kissed her
Till he found she was dead.

Then dropping her down
To his uncle he run.
For woe and good lasses,
I've killed poor Polly Bam.

O uncle, O uncle,
What shall I do?
For woe and good lasses,
I've killed poor Polly Bam.

Her white apron over her shoulder,
I took her for a swan.
But woe and good lasses,
It was poor Polly Bam.

Stay in your own country
And don't run away.
Though woe and good lasses,
It was poor Polly Bam.

The day before trial
The ladies all appeared in a row.
Polly Bam 'peared among them
Like a fountain of snow.

Don't hang Jimmy Daniels,
For he's not to blame.
My white apron over my shoulder
He took me for a swan;
But woe and good lasses,
It was me, poor Polly Bam.

Molly Bawn

Come all you young fowlers who carry a gun.
Don't ever go a-shooting by the setting of the sun.
I was once a brave young fowler, as you may understand.
And I shot my own true love, I took her for a fawn.

She was going to her uncle when the rain it came on.
She went under a tree for to let the rain pass.
With her apron all around her, I took her for a fawn.
Oh, I never would have shot my own Molly Bawn.

And when he came to her, and found it was she.
His limbs, they were shaking, his eyes could not see.
His heart it was broken with sorrow and with grief.
And he implored up to heaven to give him relief.

Young Jimmy went home with his gun in his hand,
Saying, "Father, dearest Father, I have done what's wrong.
With her apron all around her, I took her for a fawn.
Oh, alas, and alas, I shot my Molly Bawn."

I wrapped her fair temples, and found she was dead.
A torrent of tears for my true love I shed.
And now I'll be forced by the laws of the land,
For the killing of my darling, my trial for to stand.

And the day of her funeral, her spirit it appeared,
Saying, "Uncle, dearest Uncle, do not hang my dear.
With my apron all around me, he took me for a fawn
Oh, he never would have shot his own Molly Bawn."

Silver Dagger

Come all young men, please lend attention
To these few words I'm going to write;
They are as true as ever were written
Concerning a lady fair and bright.

A young man courted a fair young maiden;
He loved her as he loved his life,
And always vowed that he would make her
His own true and wedded wife.

But when his parents came to know this,
They tried to part them day and night,
Saying, "Son, O son, don't you be so foolish -
That girl's too poor for to be your wife."

This young man fell down on his knees a-pleading,
"O father, mother, pity me.
Don't take from me my dearest darling,
For she is all the world to me."

But when the young lady came to know this,
She soon resolved what she would do.
She wandered forth and from the city,
Never more her charms to view.

She wandered down by a bright flowing river,
And sat herself beneath a tree.
She sighed and said, "O will I ever,
Will I e'er more my true love see?"

Then up she picked her silver dagger,
And pressed it through her snowy white breast.
She first did reel and then did stagger,
Saying, "My true love, you come too late."

This young man being by the roadside heard her;
He thought he knew his true love's voice.
He ran, he ran, like one distracted,
Saying, "My true love, I fear you're lost."

He ran up to this dying body,
Rolled it over into his arms,
Saying, "Neither gold nor friends can save you,
For you are dying in my arms."

Her two pretty eyes like stars she opened,
Saying, "My true love, you come too late.
Prepare to meet me on Mount Zion,
Where all lovers' joys shall be complete."

Then up he picked this bloody dagger,
Pressed it through his aching heart;
And now, dear friends, may this be a warning
To all who try true love to part.

Katie Dear

"O Katie Dear, go ask your father
If you may be a bride of mine;
If he says No, please come and tell me;
And I'll no longer trouble you."

"O Willie dear, it's no use to ask him.
He's in his room and taking his rest.
By his side a golden dagger
To kill the one that I love best."

"O Katie dear, go ask your mother
If you may be a bride of mine;
If she says No, please come and tell me;
And I'll no longer trouble you."

"O Willie dear, it's no use to ask her.
She's in her room and taking her rest.
By her side a silver dagger
To kill the one that I love best."

O he picked up a silver dagger,
He pierced it through his wounded breast.
"Farewell, Katy, farewell, darling,
I'll die for the one that I love best."

She picked up the bloody weapon,
She pierced it through her snow-white breast.
"Farewell, mamma, farewell papa,
I'll go with the one that I love best."

Cumberland Gap

Molly the mare led a quiet life
Until that bay caused her woeful strife.
Woeful strife. Woeful strife.
Until that bay caused her woeful strife.

Johnny Oxford a sad young chap,
Lost his grip in Cumberland Gap.
Cumberland Gap. Cumberland Gap.
Lost his grip in Cumberland Gap.

Polly Vaughn was a beautiful girl.
Showed true love afor she left this world.
Left this world. Left this world.
Showed true love afor she left this world.

Johnson Boys loved to fish and trap.
Got caught themselves in Cumberland Gap.
Cumberland Gap. Cumberland Gap.
Got caught themselves in Cumberland Gap.

Big John's hammer his chains did mock.
Rang out freedom on Pinnacle Rock.
Pinnacle Rock. Pinnacle Rock.
Rang out freedom on Pinnacle Rock.

Katy dear loved Willie Moore.
Together now for evermore.
Evermore. Evermore.
Together now for evermore.

Donal Daley made a mountain dew.
Them refusin' were mighty few.
Mighty few. Mighty few.
Them refusin' were mighty few.

Me, my wife and my wife's pap
Lived and loved in Cumberland Gap.
Cumberland Gap. Cumberland Gap.
Lived and loved in Cumberland Gap.